# ASSAULT ON SUNRISE

BOOKS BY MICHAEL SHEA

*A Quest for Simbilis*
*Nifft the Lean*
*The Color Out of Time*
*In Yana, the Touch of Undying*
*Fat Face*
*I, Said the Fly*
*Polyphemus*
*The Mines of Behemoth*
*The Incompleat Nifft*
*The A'Rak*
*The Extra**
*Assault on Sunrise**
*Fortress Hollywood* (forthcoming)*
*The Autopsy and Other Tales*
*Copping Squid and Other Mythos Tales*

*A Tom Doherty Associates Book

# ASSAULT ON SUNRISE

**MICHAEL SHEA**

A TOM DOHERTY ASSOCIATES BOOK
**NEW YORK**

This is a work of fiction. All of the characters, organizations, and events portrayed in this novel are either products of the author's imagination or are used fictitiously.

ASSAULT ON SUNRISE



Map by Jon Lansberg

Edited by James Frenkel

A Tor Book
Published by Tom Doherty Associates, LLC
175 Fifth Avenue
New York, NY 10010

www.tor-forge.com



Library of Congress Cataloging-in-Publication Data

Shea, Michael, 1946–
Assault on sunrise / Michael Shea. — First edition.
pages cm
"A Tom Doherty Associates book."
ISBN 978-0-7653-2436-8 (hardcover)
ISBN 978-1-4299-8827-8 (e-book)
1. Motion pictures—Fiction. 2. Extras (Actors)—Fiction. 3. Adventure fiction. I. Title.
PS3619.H3998A88 2013
813'.6—dc23

2013015149

Tor books may be purchased for educational, business, or promotional use. For information on bulk purchases, please contact Macmillan Corporate and Premium Sales Department at 1-800-221-7945 extension 5442 or write specialmarkets@macmillan.com.

First Edition: August 2013

Printed in the United States of America

0 9 8 7 6 5 4 3 2 1

*As always, to Linda*

Trinity Mountains

1 Cinnabar Tavern
2 *Dead Cat Alley*
3 Library
4 *Smelter Alley*
5 Lumber Yards
6 Sawmill
7 West Glacier
8 Dead Laid Here
9 Masonic Building / Basement Workshop
10 Cap's Hardware
11 Machine Shop
12 Automotive Shop
13 Hydroponic Hank's
14 *Back Alley*
15 *Water Street*
16 *South Bridge*
17 *Live Oak Road*
18 *North Street*
19 Oak Barrel Bar
20 Ike's Engine Repair
21 *Ike's Alley*
22 Wheel Right Hogs
23 Cuppa Joe

34

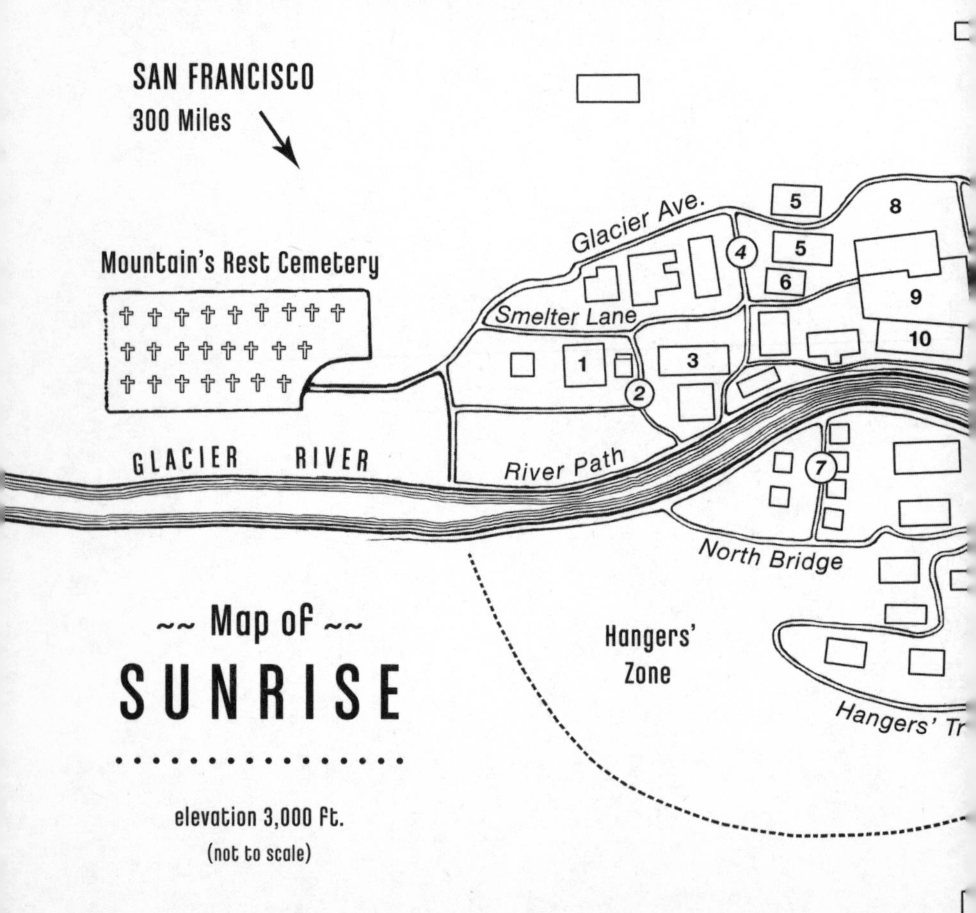

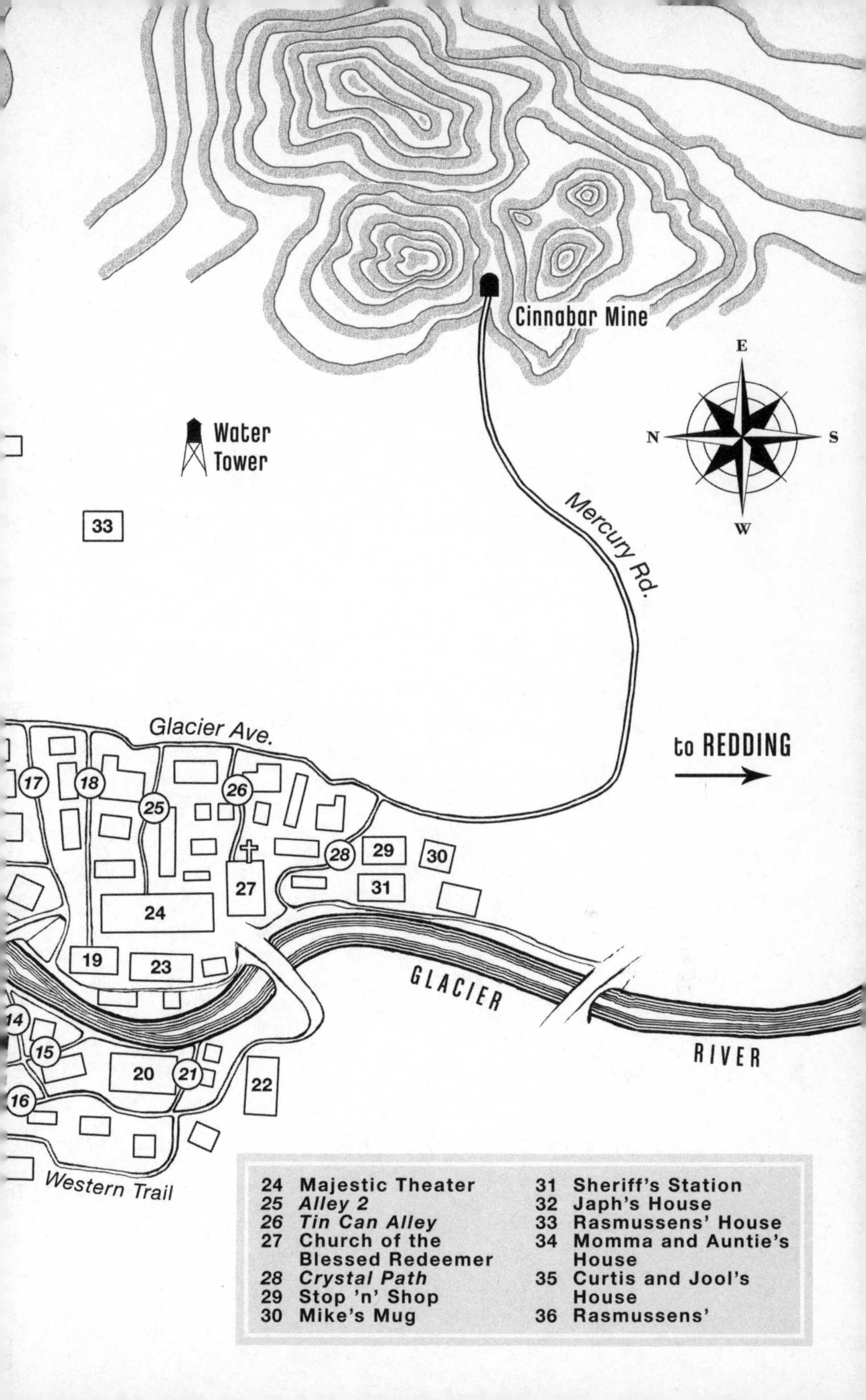
Cinnabar Mine
E
N
S
W
Water Tower
33
Mercury Rd.
to REDDING
Glacier Ave.
17
18
25
26
27
28
29
30
31
24
19
23
GLACIER
RIVER
14
15
20
21
22
16
Western Trail
24 Majestic Theater
25 Alley 2
26 Tin Can Alley
27 Church of the Blessed Redeemer
28 Crystal Path
29 Stop 'n' Shop
30 Mike's Mug
31 Sheriff's Station
32 Japh's House
33 Rasmussens' House
34 Momma and Auntie's House
35 Curtis and Jool's House
36 Rasmussens'

# ASSAULT ON SUNRISE

# CHANCE

**As the late** summer sun neared setting, Jool was working on their winter garden. Curtis came back up from town, two rolls of chicken wire in the little bed of their three-wheeler. He paused just shy of their house, an A-frame cabin they'd finished at last in just under two years. Paused because, in town, he'd heard news he didn't want to tell her.

She was weeding, her face profiled in the golden light that shadowed the honey-colored slant of her cheekbones. He could see the low swelling of her belly, like the curve of a crescent moon. Four months along. Their baby would be a beautiful blend—his black with her buckskin hues; his frame solid, hers slender.

"Guess what." she called. "We've got a visitor." Though she said it smiling, there was something sad in her eyes.

"Someone I know?"

"I think so. In a way." And here the visitor came, loping down the path behind her: a rangy dog, vaguely Lab-shaped with longish blond fur. A big, affable fellow, all tongue and enthusiasm.

And the moment Curtis saw it, he understood what he'd seen in Jool's face. In a heartbeat he was projected back to that morning in L.A., sitting with thousands of other extras-to-be in the bleachers outside Panoply Studio's great wall, watching a demo of the monsters they would be facing on the set inside that wall. They'd watched a dog that looked very much like this one come to a gruesome end.

"Damn," he said.

"Yeah."

Faces and memories. Their thoughts went inward to fugues of nightmare and adrenalized turmoil they would never forget. It came naturally, then, for Curtis to tell her what he had just learned in town.

She stroked his face and sighed. The sun was just set. Below them Sunrise, in its tree line, had its streetlights on. "I'll tell Momma and your Auntie Drew," she said. The house they had built for those two ladies was just in the next vale over from their own. "You go up and tell Chops and Gillian. We'll meet you for the meeting down in the hall. And this guy? We'll keep him, right?"

"Sure."

She smiled. "You sure now? He's a big eater—already finished the rest of last night's roast."

He smiled back. "What do you want to call him?"

"Well, he was lucky to find us," she said. "Let's call him Chance."

# STARRY NIGHT

**Up in the** Trinity Mountains, the stars—even when the quarter moon was up—were no feeble thing. The universe was right there on top of you, a pavement of white coals. Their light lay like frost on the grassy slopes and on the grandfather pines in their thousands.

As Gillian bent to the eyepiece of their telescope, Chops watched her, her Native American hair a black so glossy that the stars struck gleams off it.

"Whoa . . ." she said softly, and Chops, seeing her so tenderly intent, felt a tingle of warmth.

Raising her head, she beckoned him and whispered—as if they must be careful not to disturb the distant galaxy she had just captured for them. "Take a look."

And peering at it, he in his turn had to say, "Whoa." It was a tiny egg of light, fuzzy round its edges with a fog of stars: the globular cluster in Orion's sword.

Gillian, as much Comanche as Miwok, had grown up on one rez after another in Idaho, Washington, and here in Northern California—drifting with different branches of family, with friends—always preferring to live in mountains and forests on their own terms and nowhere bulldozers had made.

Sometimes she'd think of Chops as a wolf who was also her mate. A lean, smallish one, rapt now by this lens on the stars, but always ready to jump at a sound or a scent. She wanted to stroke the bristly fur on the back of his head, but held back so as not to risk startling him.

He'd been born in the Zoo, a hard life in itself. Then he'd been to prison and there suffered scars one couldn't see. He would never hurt her, but loving him she never touched him unaware.

"Jeez!" he said. "Stars! I never saw them in L.A."

Gillian had quested in three different mountain ranges through the years of her adolescence. She knew how to fast and find that ghostly unity with the wilderness where hunger and physical extremity made your senses pour out of you like radiation, where all life's personalities—clawed, fanged, feathered, scaled, and furred—sooner or later showed themselves. Where they met your eyes and let you look into theirs.

Once, a few years ago, a cougar, a well-grown female, came stepping onto a game trail she'd sat by. Such was the big cat's beauty that when it left, Gillian believed that her wonder had canceled her fear and purchased her life.

Chops's first quest had begun at sunup yesterday morning five miles higher in the mountains. They had reached the place where they were to diverge—for each one's vigil must be alone. A deer trail crossed a steep open field of brush and lupen amid spruce forest.

Chops had tried to clarify his feelings toward the quest he was embracing. "I do feel open to all the living things here, but you know I'm armed." He touched the hilt at the small of his back, his one knife, almost a short-sword. "I can't help it. I just won't go unarmed anywhere there's a chance I might have to protect you."

"Honey," she said. "Everyone does it their own way."

Sitting there a while before parting, just in the pleasure of being together, they could smell the lupen and ferns all around them and the forest-scent washing over them in the breeze. They watched the greens get greener, the sky bluer. The pine skirts crowding the path gave a shudder . . . and a big brown bear, five hundred pounds at least, came rolling forward.

Gillian knew her for a sow. Worse luck if she had cubs still trailing her—spring was not terribly far behind them after all. No cubs appeared, but the bear paused just before them. Chops seemed to find amazing depths in her little muddy reddish eyes. To Gillian's eyes, in that moment, Chops seemed to have borrowed some of the animal's magnificence.

The bear seemed to see only him, to find something absorbing in that rapt human form. She seemed not to register the disparity between her mass and his. And then with a direct glance at last to Gillian—a glance oddly like a courteous parting nod—the sow had turned and padded on up the trail.

Maybe it wasn't a proper vision quest. Could you have a joint vision quest? They'd been talking it over since yesterday.

Now, as she was pointing out for Chops the Pleiades, her com purred. She clicked it on, listened, and murmured, "OK. We're coming down."

"What's up?" Chops asked.

"Curtis is coming to meet us. There's a big meeting, some kinda bad news."

They capped the telescope and folded its little tripod slowly, still looking up at the stars. They wanted to stay in the peaks, not go down to the valley. But they also knew that if it was the town's trouble, it had to be theirs too.

Coming the last half mile downslope, the couple paused to look at Sunrise. All the lights of the town were burning, the broad main drag the brightest. The half-dozen branch roads that angled up and downslope of its axis showed lesser lights—glowing windows and porch lights, some yards floodlit to protect gardens from deer and chicken coops from foxes. The whole looked like a jagged little lightning-bolt beneath the starry night.

They paused when they reached the tall new water tower, which marked the town's upslope rim. Between it and Glacier Avenue spread an industrial fringe of wide lots and hangar-like buildings of various sizes—two lumberyards, a sawmill, a couple machine shops, the automotive repair shop with trouble lights glaring from raised hoods.

Curtis emerged from one of the alleys off Glacier and came across the weedy crackled asphalt to meet them.

"Sorry to drag you down," he said. He hugged them.

"What's up?" asked Chops.

"It all happened yesterday, and happened pretty fast. A group of guys came looking for the Rasmussens. Armed guys. And as you'd expect, some of those guys got shot. And, as it turns out, those dead guys are state cops." Curtis let them take this in.

All Chops said quietly was, "Shit." But Gillian knew what her mate was thinking. What they were all thinking. Just how far away do you have to go to be free?

"We're about on time," Curtis told them. "Smalls is gonna make his report." He slanted them a look, and they could see his grin in the mix of starlight and streetlights just ahead of them.

"You know, you guys look good. Did you see anything?"

Chops smiled. "Funny you should ask."

# TOWN MEETING

**They'd never seen** the Majestic this full—a quarter of the town must have been there. The movie-house seating was long gone. A half acre of folding chairs, stools, armchairs, and anything else that could be sat on filled the floor, with just crooked pathways branching between them. The tattered screen was still hanging in place, and the low dais in front of it was where Sheriff Smalls now stood waiting for the uproar to die down so he could speak.

Everyone was roaring at once. It was a motley mob Smalls faced, maybe six hundred souls. The majority were second and third generation mountain-born, and these ranged from sheep ranchers in boots and canvas coats, to machinists and lumber-millers in denim and leather, to bikers in leathers with rabid wolves painted on them. Mixed in were the town's white-collar folks in neat flannel shirts and pressed jeans.

Then there were the relative newcomers to Sunrise, mostly ex-extras like Curtis. Most of these, unlike Curtis, had been Zoo, and hadn't stopped looking it. Though interspersed with the natives, they were easy to spot, because down in the Zoo, flair is an issue. They had neck tats that put Curtis's little necklace of blood-drops to shame: barbed wire, ouroboroses, battling squids and dragons wrapped their throats and branched down along their spines. Hair was anything, or half scalp tats, or nothing. Earrings were big—and sometimes *big*—usually of fierce ugly things devouring their own tails. Nose rings, lip rings clung to faces like crescent moons of gold or platinum. Denim vests tattered from wear bore on their backs demons in gorgeous brocade. Knives hung sheathed behind shoulders, and on some knuckles chromium impactors were implanted.

In all this hubbub Smalls, bulky and half bald, just stood on the dais facing the crowd, his big face slack and shoulders slumped. He made Curtis think of a chained bear, duty-bound to hear, humor, and help if he could this mad mob.

He caught Curtis's eye, and shouted something twice before Curtis understood and went and closed the old theater's doors.

Smalls' mouth worked for a while, completely inaudible.

Then he shouted. Then he really shouted, and everyone decided to shut up and listen.

"People . . . everyone's been commed. I want as many as possible to hear it together and get some kinda consensus, so that everyone else gets the full picture straight.

"Now for shit-sake don't interrupt me, please! Lemme lay the whole thing out, because it's the whole thing needs talking through, because we are lookin at a serious disaster." New shouts, questions, but just as quick, more voices shushed them. Smalls took a deep breath.

"Yesterday morning six strangers came into town while I was down-county on business. They showed up in pairs in different parts of town, but they were all eggs from the same basket. They all wore up-woods clothes brand-new, synthetic down vests, big new hiking boots, excetera. Four of 'em had face hair, but so barbered it looked just as store-bought as their rigs.

"They went everywhere. In all the bars, all the shops, even the public library. They asked all kinda sly and under-the-table where they could find a man named Elmer Rasmussen. Like it was a mystery."

That woke some laughter. Any time after 3:00 P.M., Old Elmer would be down in one of the town's three bars. Not a sot, just a reliable drinker once sundown hove anywhere in sight. Somber Elmer—sitting now right below the dais—ignored the laughter.

"The result," said Smalls, "was that everybody they asked said they didn't know any such fella. Then at least twenty of those people went right up to Elmer's afterward and told him that some strange goons were in town lookin for him.

"Around eleven A.M. Hap Bolger came up half drunk from Shasta, said sure he knew Elmer, and told them where his house was.

"So. The six of those city boys came up on Elmer's house and stood fanned out in front of it. Their jackets were open and they all had industrial-grade firearms in shoulder rigs showing, but they weren't showin any I.D. Elmer stepped out on the porch. He had on a jacket but—I guess ten a.m. was kinda early by his standards—was wearing just his boxers."

A female voice crowed out, "Oh Elmer! I sure wish I coulda seen those bony white legs a yours!"

"Elmer was unarmed," Smalls went on evenly. "But he had three of his sons an' four of his grandkids all standing at the front windows on either side of him, and all of them were holdin firearms.

"The lead city boy stepped out an' told Elmer that him and his brother Rake were under arrest, Rake for murder and Elmer for accessory."

"That's a load a horseshit!" roared Elmer Rasmussen, brought out of his brooding by the sense of injustice that seethed in him. "Rake cut that guy with the guy's own knife after he'd stuck it into Rake first! An' they both walked away!—well, limped away maybe."

"Guy just died," said Smalls.

"More'n a year later!"

"We know it's bullshit, Elmer!" shouted Smalls. "That's

my point! Just lemme tell everyone, OK? Anyway. Who opened fire first? Who knows? Once you got this kinda situation, someone's gonna fire an' everyone else's gonna follow.

"Now the first important point for everyone to notice comes right here." Smalls scratched his right arm, an older style motorized prosthetic, which of course never really itched—the scratching a tic of his when he was trying to sort out problems. "Body armor and all, three of those six fellas were riddled with thirty-ought and were dead or dyin before any of 'em caught on that their own guns weren't doin anything. I want you to notice this point, folks. They obviously thought they had solid rounds. They were issued bogus ammo an' didn't know they were shooting powdered lead!

"The three who weren't drilled yet took off when it dawned on 'em, commed down a jet-sled from somewhere, and were snatched off the mountain a hundred meters downslope. The only killing they'd managed was of three of themselves. They hit Elmer center-mass, and just gave him some big bruises."

"They nearly took one a my eyes!" Elmer turned his gaunt, outraged face full on the rest of the audience for the first time. It wore an accent mark of thick red scab where half of his left eyebrow had once dangled its shaggy abundance. Amazed, aggrieved, he said, "They fuckin disfigured me!"

"Anyway," resumed Smalls, "after the shoot-out we found that the three dead ones did in fact have state licenses on 'em and had the murder warrant. And now Sunrise is 'corporately accused' of three counts of homicide. That means all of us, individually accused. Of aggravated homicide against state officers of the peace in performance of their duty—a top-of-the-list capital offense."

Smalls' eyes swept the audience. "It seems to me pretty damn plain that all of us have just been framed. That those guys had blanks to ensure that they'd die. We've already been informed that the state has enough camera footage of the shoot-out for its so-called 'deliberations.' That raft that picked up the survivors must've been shootin the whole damn thing! But the short of it is, they've informed me—and I quote—that 'the murder charge will be adjudicated unilaterally by the state.' We should have a ruling in two to three days."

Everyone's voices woke up again, but the noise had a deeper pitch. Doubt and dread could be heard in it. Their voices churned like choppy seas, till someone stood up with the lungs to be heard.

"Why?" It was Cap. He stepped up on the platform.

Not quite Curtis's height, but more heavily muscled, his and Japh's Zoo-meat friend had bloomed up here in the mountains. He'd bought the hardware store when they all first arrived, and for all his Zoo toughness he loved being a shopkeeper.

His cue-ball head shone in the warmth of the jammed room. "Sheriff's right, we've been flat-out framed. And it makes no sense! Why would the state wanna destroy us? I mean money-wise? We're a thriving economy. State scarfs on our sales an' income taxes, on the power they sell us.

"There was Cranktown, sure, but that was just trash-clearing, demolition. Nothing but shoot-outs an' untaxable drug money. But why trash the cash they're raking off us?"

Cranktown in San Berdoo was a statewide surprise. Not because the state had sent contract-cops into that hive, but because when some of these cops got shot it charged Cranktown, Inc. corporately with homicide, and inflicted "in-field capital punishment" on more than half of them. Jailed the rest and made their site state property—and a trashy, polluted piece it was.

Sunrise was an earning concern. Incorporated Rural Townships (IRTs) like Sunrise policed and fire-protected themselves, built their own roads and infrastructure, bought power from the state, and paid hefty taxes. Organic veggies, meat and dairy, natural textiles, specialty lumber, quality weed—all these sold as luxuries on the Coast.

Curtis stood up. "The state's got us. But you wonder. Was it the state's idea? I gotta tell you I don't like bringing this up. I and a lot of my fellow ex-extras up here, well . . . we just hate this happening to everyone here, who took us in as neighbors. But it has to be said: Why the hell would the state frame a whole community like this? I hate saying this—you have no idea how bad it makes me feel—but what if it's really a studio that's behind this?"

Not everyone got this at first. A growl of conversation began to fill the theater. Sandy Devlin stood up. That's all this hot-dog ex-payboat rafter from Panoply Studios had to do to get everyone's attention. "Can I come up, Sheriff? You mind?"

"How could we mind?"

# IV

## I HOPE TO GOD WE'RE WRONG

**Sandy Devlin mounted** the dais. Not willingly, but since she felt herself and other ex-Studio folk to be on the spot, she figured she might as well stand there. Before her now—she struggled to suppress the thought—there sat so many of the dead-to-be. She scanned their faces, trying to meet all of them eye to eye. Seeing ghosts-to-be, she found, led to seeing ghosts that had been.

A lean, bright-haired woman. Even with her eyes looking somewhat at a loss, her body was restlessly present, her weight shifting left leg to right and back again. "Give me a second," she told the packed room. All her years of payboating for the studios were suddenly upon her, a fugue of images, of people dying in agony beneath her on the teeming pavements of a dozen different sets.

So many shapes of violent death, reaping a mad harvest of souls, their whole lives left down there, sprawled in that broken meat. For years her only help for them was paying fast, shouting warnings. Later she'd defended them, covertly killing APPs where she could. She could have quit. But then there wouldn't have been even one raft to help them.

But look what she'd paid for staying in the game. How clear and individual those faces, hundreds of them, in her brain forever. Desperate people making their lives' one big gamble and losing it, and taking in rage and grief the last look at the sky they'd ever get. The sky that she zipped through untouched.

She found she had to clear her throat before speaking. "I don't know how it happened, but I've never thanked you, all of you, for taking me in here, me and the friends who came with me." She paused again, but it had to be spoken. "I hope to god we haven't somehow brought this here."

"Nonsense!" An indignant old lady's voice. She was in a motor-operated wheelchair with a high wooden back to it, like a judge's chair. Iris Meyer, retired teacher of the Sunrise Grammar School. Three generations of grown Sunrise natives had been schooled and scolded by her through grades four to six. She glared around, a woman who had no problem talking to crowds. "Evil doesn't need to be brought anywhere. It comes calling on its own." A lot of the native

Sunrisers' heads, gray ones among them, listened slightly bowed in an ancient reflex of obedience and attention. "I don't know about the rest of you"—a pause here just long enough to have added "boys and girls"—"but when evil comes here to my home, it's going to have me to deal with."

This brief declaration felt like a hand on Sandy's shoulder. She cleared her throat. "Thank you, Iris. Friends, those who don't want to stay, we'll get you out. We'll get you safe. For those who are staying . . . I'm not gonna say what I suspect. Not till I know for sure. I just wanna emphasize what Sheriff Smalls has already shown us: how . . . skillfully this whole thing was scripted. Six dip-sticks in phony costumes, with low social skills, perfectly cast to irritate and alarm everyone. And sent here for the Rasmussens. No offense, Elmer—we all respect you—but you and your family have been involved in more 'firearm incidents' than any twenty other families put together."

Some chuckles here—some from the younger Rasmussens themselves.

"So. Look at it, friends. Perfectly scripted. The goons to alienate and threaten. The Rasmussens to return fire. This script worked like a charm, and we are corporately incriminated in first degree murder. And Cap's exactly right. Is it likely the state wants title to our land? To our modest lumber output? Our alpaca flocks or livestock bloodlines? Our low-yield cinnabar mine? What's left for them to want here, except our bodies? Except us? And of course, the state can't want those either. If we're evicted, or if we're corpses, the state loses taxes. If we're in prison, the state's supporting us.

"So it's plain as day. This isn't coming from state. It's someone who has the money to buy a murder warrant from the right corrupt people in state government."

That caused a silence in the hall about three heartbeats long. Someone tall stood up—it was Japh. "Tell me if I'm off here, Sandy. If Sunrise is found guilty, the state can license any body of state approved corp-cops to enforce the sentence on us."

"Correct. That's the next step. And of course any sizeable corporation will have its own licensed enforcement arm. So. What corporation might want to own us?"

She paused—felt the silent attention from these endangered hundreds. Steady, stubborn people, living their own ways and accepting one another's. It dawned on her: she loved them. Straight-up, generous people. Even with this danger upon them, there seemed to be no rancor turned toward the extras.

"You might already get what I personally believe. But ask all your Coast contacts, get them to put their ears to the vine. Myself, I'm going down to L.A."

Low talk started here and there, and quickly rose back to a roar. Sandy stepped off the platform and made for the doors, but a lot of people wanted to show her solidarity—gripped her hands or smacked her shoulders. She was dying to get out those big double doors and into the night by herself.

"Sandy's right," Ricky Dawes told Japh and Curtis. "Something rotten here. Government—that's something you can always buy if you have the clacks." Ricky had been in his sawmill the last ten hours, was hungry, and his thoughts were tending toward his lunch bag. Japh jumped to his feet and gripped both his friends' shoulders. "We going to meet up at Chops and Gilly's?"

"Naw, not me," said Ricky. "I got more paneling to mill. Then I gotta get down to the Valley early, get plenty of twelve-gauge shells."

Curtis said, "We'll bring up beer, Japh. Eleven or so!"

Because Japh was already edging his way through the crowd toward the doors that Sandy had just gone out of.

**"Sandy! Wait!" She** was already two blocks down Glacier Avenue, and just hooking into an alley where her two-seater Jag was parked, when Japh's shout stopped her.

In the alley mouth she stood half in shadow, while Japh stood full in the streetlight. He looked at her, earnest, a little hesitant.

"Just lemme do something, Sandy. It'll just take a second."

He ducked in quick and kissed her cheek. "I wanna tell ya, like, you're dear to me. You're dear to a lotta people."

It seemed perfectly natural, then, that she should stand there grinning up at him. It was like she'd known him all her life, and could even see in his somewhat scuffed-up face the happy, disaster-prone kid he'd been when he was ten—just as if they had been kids together.

She said, "Gimme your face a minute," reaching up and

taking his head in her hands and bringing it down to where she could thrust up her own and rub her cheek against his. It made her laugh, it felt so satisfying.

"I think," he said, "I'm afraid I know why you're going to L.A."

"Yeah . . ."

"I hope to God we're wrong."

**Smalls had opened** the platform for people to speak by turn. Dozens jumped to their feet and, while waiting to be called on, began talking in a deafening roar, so the sheriff had to bellow, "Shut up please! By turns. Christy. You speak first."

A slight young man, with short white-blond hair. He was one of the bikers from down at the Wheel Right Hogs. "I say it's first things first. We hafta get everyone properly armed."

Others followed Christy. Two-thirds agreed with him, but differed at length about armaments. The other third repetitively suggested that the whole town take to the higher mountains, or down to stay with friends in the Valley, in Redding or Red Bluff or fucking Sacramento.

So much repetition quickly bored Ricky Dawes. He slipped his hard-callused hand into his lunch bag and unwrapped his sandwich. He'd been cooped up all day milling a big order for new residents—a bunch of just-arrived survivors from *Maw of Mars.* Ricky was a gnarly middleweight pushing forty, a man with an incessant appetite who would die lean through no fault of his own. He'd brooded all he could about Sunrise's dire straits, and was tired of thinking about it now.

He tucked in and enjoyed it—pork and dill pickles on rye bread. . . . And as he ate, his idle eye kept noticing one of the dogs at the meeting.

A few older people had to have their dogs for support or guidance, and at every meeting there were always some people straight down from the hills at work who brought their dogs with them, always on sufferance for good behavior. Thus a substantial canine presence marked all meetings in the Hall with a family mood. But this particular dog, a biggish black-Lab mix, had a stand-out quality that Ricky couldn't quite put his finger on.

It was an unusually clean dog, for one thing. For another, it threaded here and there through the crooked aisles among the crowd, very active and alert but seemingly not after anything—acting exploratory and curious in the general way of dogs, but casual about it, not really hunting human touches or acknowledgment.

When it trotted past Ricky on its circuit, he held out a chunk of his sandwich to it. It gave the treat a dab of its nose, and trotted by. Ricky was startled when Iris Meyer on his left said, "Where are all these new dogs coming from lately?"

"All what dogs, Miz Iris?"

"All the new ones around!" She answered in a testy tone that seemed to add, 'you young airhead!' "There's that little Sheltie mix. And the first time I saw that wooly brown bitch over there was yesterday."

"Sorry, Miz Iris. I don't get outta my mill much during the days. I guess dogs wander in, what can you say?"

"No they don't, Richard Dawes." Her tone induced meek attention from Ricky, and she went on to describe three other canine newcomers she had seen around town. And after a moment it struck Ricky . . . that she was right. Few strange dogs did wander in to any settled community like this, as full as it was of territorial resident dogs.

"Listen, people," shouted Smalls, whom the endless, aimless series of speakers had at last exhausted. "We're spinning our wheels. The charge is gonna be judged without us, and damn small doubt of the verdict. Go talk to everyone else now! Network! Go city-side, coast-side, find out what you can about who's after us.

"But I just wanna say one last thing for myself. This situation we've got hasn't changed one thing for me. When I went extra on *They Teem,* I went in knowin already that Sunrise here was where I wanted to buy in, where I wanted to live. An since I've been here, it's been worth every ounce of the arm it cost me. I'm not goin anywhere else. Anyone comes to cage or kill me had best bring their lunch, and all the help they can find.

"So. Tomorrow at my office we'll be organizing runs down to the Valley, both for those who are . . . relocating temporarily, and for those who are setting in stores. Com or come in and we'll try to get everyone taken care of."

**As the moon** declined, they all sat on Chops and Gillian's deck under the star-ceiling, which shed light enough to make their eyes glint from their shadowed sockets. All except Jool were holding a beer or a second beer. Curtis and Jool sat at the deck's edge dangling their legs off, arms around each other's shoulders.

Gillian said, "If you count people who are older but still tight, we could have six or seven hundred effectives up here."

"More!" said Chops. "And a lot are way-back country people who know how to fight." They were looking far down the slope at Sunrise, whose jagged lines of street and house lights was a tiny echo of the stars' abundance.

Gillian said, "Whoever's doing this, they have to know that a lot of people are gonna fight. I think the fight is probably what they want."

Japh said, edging closer to it with the rest of them, "The scam that got us in this fix . . . was really well scripted."

Japh noted that Curtis and Jool's embrace got a little closer as they looked down over the town. Curtis nodded.

"It's pretty clear Sandy's not just going to L.A.—she's going to Hollywood."

Now it was out. They all relaxed a little.

"Real-life Live Action," Japh said bitterly. "Another groundbreaker. And who's the biggest groundbreaker of them all? Who invented Live Action?"

"Gotta be," Chops growled. "You know there're two hundred survivors just from *Alien Hunger* alone up here?"

"Yeah. Has to be Panoply Studios Sandy's got in mind."

# V
# TARGET PRACTICE

**Before the sun** came up, Curtis and Jool woke up and got it on. As their baby had grown in her, he had taken to moving more gingerly when he was in her too, worried that it might hurt Jool to be holding them both. But then she began to ride him strongly, snatching him up into her recklessness and making him reckless too.

Reckless was good, because it was like a promise. It meant they had their whole lives of love ahead of them and could spend it how they wanted. He felt that she was not riding toward him, but taking the three of them away from here to somewhere safe from what was coming down.

Afterward, embraced, their heartbeats slowing, it seemed they had indeed traveled and passed a long and happy time somewhere else. But here came the real world gathering around them once more, the dangerous world they'd lived in since the day before yesterday.

He put his hand on her belly. "Jool. Would you please just go? Get the baby, get Momma and Auntie far away and safe? You know me—no way I won't survive and bring you all back here!"

"Honey," she said, "you wouldn't go, if it was just you. I wouldn't go, if it was just me. And you and me are who this baby's gotta live with. Down in the Zoo I dreamt all my life of a place like this. Nothing's gonna chase me out of it."

"What about Auntie and Momma? They're spry but they're not young."

She smiled. "We can ask 'em to go—do you see 'em doin it?"

They lay stroking each other, the sky's silver light like warm drapery on them. Their love began growing again as they fondled and snuggled, involved in that sweet studious wrestling, trying to get closer, and closer still, shedding tears as they came.

After, they dozed till the sun was rising, and had just dressed and started coffee when Momma and Auntie's three-wheeler growled down the slope, coming down from The Garden Spot, their "flower ranch" two hills over, with Auntie Drew at the wheel.

On their runs down to L.A. to bring their household possessions up here to Sunrise, Momma Grace had proved to be God's own combat-driver when running the Five through the bandit nests, but lately she'd been putting Curtis's auntie at the wheel to train her. Auntie's fingers, crooked from years of keyboarding in the 'Rise, were straighter already with her months of gardening, and she loved driving, but that hadn't made her very good at it yet. Fearless and enthusiastic, yes—and this could make her dangerous if you were in, or near, her path.

When the coffee was ready they brought it out to the ladies, who were just coming up the steps. They all talked planting and fertilizers, gulping the brew.

When Jool and Curtis had at last made their pitch, Auntie squawked, "Run us down to Redding? Curtis, you must be trippin! We're stayin right here, an we mean to cap some studio ass, child." Her diction had gone downhill up here in Sunrise, even as her fingers and her spine had grown straighter. Her hair was a weedy white 'fro now, like a dandelion puffball. Momma Grace, for her part, must've lost sixty pounds—no sylph yet, but a sturdy, tight country momma.

"Well then," Jool said, "lemme get you some things we've got for you."

She brought out the weighty duffel she and Curtis had readied, and took from it first two old shirts. Foam blocks cut from an old cushion were glued inside their right shoulders. "Put these on an button 'em up, dears. Get the foam snug on the front of your shoulders. . . . Good. Now let's go on up to that draw there. We've got us some practicing to do."

Auntie asked, "Practicing what?" But her smile at the satchel said she already knew. As they marched ahead up through the grass it made Curtis sad to watch them. You could see them just loving where they were so much, the grassy hillside, the sun, and the sky.

A fold in the hillside was their destination. There was a bit of level ground in this nook and some shrubs and small trees half filled it. One big old log, a long-fallen pine, lay at a tilt in the brush, bright green moss wrapping half its bark.

"We should stand about here," Curtis told them. "And we'll do our practicing on that trunk there."

"Slip these on round your necks," Jool said, handing them earmuffs. "You'll cover your ears when you're actually firing."

Curtis took out the two sawed-off pump-actions. "Take hold of 'em like this . . . right. Now, snug the stocks against the padding on your shoulders. Here . . . like this . . ."

Maybe they sensed how it scared their "youngsters" to see them holding those little steel brutes. Momma's reversion to Zoo-talk was a match for Auntie Drew's—and she a tutor of English for so many years! "Why you puppies so long-faced?" she laughed. "You think we don' know howda stomp some? Kick-ass our middle names!"

Curtis and Jool had them dry-fire a while, perfecting their stances, left feet advanced, whole backs and hips braced against the trigger pull. Aiming, bracing, triggering, working the slide . . . "How your hands, girl?" Momma asked Auntie Drew. "They looking so strong now an' straight!"

"Thanks to you, Gracie," she answered. "Thanks to our rakes an our shovels. Hands of steel! They could snap a damn keyboard in half!"

"OK," Curtis told them, concealing a sinking feeling at this graver phase of their work here. "Now you load them like this . . . firm push with the thumb and tuck it up in there . . . right . . . OK. Five in the magazine, good. Now jack one into the chamber—pull that slide firmly, that's it—always pull that slide crisply all the way. Now, one more in the magazine. Good. Very careful from here on out, cause remember you got one in the chamber. Bring it up sure it's pointed away from anyone you don't wanna hit, because now the damn thing will fire."

Jool slipped their earmuffs on them, and then Curtis spoke louder. "Now. Lean forward and brace for the recoil and just hit that trunk, anywhere along its upper half."

Auntie would still have pitched straight over backward if Curtis hadn't stood braced right behind her. Momma Grace shouted, "Holy shit!" in happy awe at the thunder she'd unleashed.

Two dozen rounds they fired. Toward the end their aim got better and they dug a big splintery chasm in the trunk. Watching, Jool and Curtis were glad for their months in the mountains. How sturdy they'd gotten! There was a dazed, pleased look on their faces, and a pair of grins when each caught the other's eye: two ladies of some power now.

But Jool and Curtis traded a different look. Both of them were going to be in what was coming, and gone for good any chance of keeping them out of it. He saw Jool wipe her eyes quickly before she said brightly, "All right! Not too shabby. Now your sidearms—"

Auntie yelped, "What's that!?"

Curtis looked where she pointed, and then checked the hillside to see if a breeze was stirring the grass, because that thick, bright moss on the trunk was rippling.

He literally rubbed his eyes. The moss was stirring in the windless air, shuddering like the fur of some animal in the early sunlight. Shuddering and contracting, because its green pelt thickened and narrowed till it looked like a python . . . and just like a python, it reared up from the trunk in a thick, swaying stalk.

The stalk budded, massive buds that melted into focused shapes, three aliens: a cruel-beaked thing all studded with rubies that saw them; a crocodilian gnawing the air with its fanged shovel-jaws; a carnivorous ape with a triad of ironic blue eyes.

These absurdities melted back into a featureless python as fast as they'd formed. The python poured off the trunk and into the undergrowth, moving like muscle, graceful along its green length, tucking into the foliage and vanishing.

The little group stood stunned. It was cinematic, a perfect little scene they'd been snared into watching: a little bow from an alien visitor to their world.

They commed Japh and Cap and Chops, and damn quick had a lot of help searching the hills, dozens of them fanning out, rummaging through grass and shrub.

They knew they'd been mocked, two of them survivors

of *Alien Hunger* whom Val Margolian might be specially ticked at. That little demo had addressed questions he knew they were desperate to answer: what would they be facing? How could they fight it?

The answer was like some snotty magician pulling bouquets from his pockets and waving them in their faces. What will you be facing? It could be anything! Look what I can do!

Long after its futility lay heavy upon them, they kept up the search, stubbornly rummaging through grass and bush, grimly refusing to let an invader lie hidden here. For these were their hills. Their freedom, their peace was here.

And all the while they searched, something was touching and tickling their bent-over backs, a radiation sly and subtle raining down: Surveillance.

To an extent they couldn't measure, they were all had. Those who were coming for them already had them covered. Their every move? Their every syllable?

The sensation settled on all of them. Spread over three hillsides, they felt it as one. And felt too what they were deciding about it: that they could not know the answers to those questions, and so they could not let those answers matter. There was only the fight as it came upon them, and only them to wage the fight.

# VI
# HOLLYWOOD

**Panoply Studio's ace** sector-boat pilot, Lance, tugged at his short horn of waxed hair. "Don't think we haven't been asking around, Sandy. I mean before you called, even. Everyone's wondering, and no one knows zip. It's the best-kept secret in Panoply's history. Development has every angle like totally under wraps, tight as a tick's ass."

His copilot, Trek, licked down an expertly rolled tobacco "skinny" and fired it up. His "bones"—bright red tufts on his cheekbones—standing out on his inflated face, he added in a tight voice, "Even the title's a total hush-hush."

Then he *whooshed* out his smoke and passed the skinny to Lance.

They sat on the deck by the pilots' pool. Their house was in the Hollywood Hills, and they gazed out over the Basin at a sky smogged its usual violet-gray.

Sandy was shaking her head. "You've gotta be shitting me—no hints at all?" If anyone had scuttlebutt it would be these two ace sector-boat pilots.

"Nope," said Trek. "You got Mark Millar setting up *Quake* on the main lot. All the other lots are tied up with this an' that. Whatever Val's doin—an word is he's doin something—it's gotta be off-set, which is like, unheard of."

"If it's sure he's doing something," Sandy said grimly, "then sure as shit, he's shooting it at Sunrise. We spanked his ass bad on *Hunger*, and now he means to eat us alive up there and get the vid as he does it. Gimme one of those brews."

As Sandy took her first sip of beer, she gazed at them thoughtfully. She knew they'd started as payboaters for Colossal, aces both. Then Panoply lured them aboard with fat contracts to fly sector boats. These were two young men who'd gone for the gold, but were still high-speed hot dogs at heart. Look at them, on their third beers already—drinking and toking, drinking and toking, their lean, restless bodies dying for action.

"Can I ask you guys a question?"

"When you ask us if you can ask us something, Devlin," Lance said, "we start thinking, Oh shit, what now?"

"Well. Your jobs seem secure at Panoply, but are you

sure Margolian's not secretly holding something against you, like letting me get away with what I did on *Hunger*?"

"Who can ever be sure what Val knows or doesn't? I'll tell you though, all the fast ones you were pulling in the last hour of that shoot, they were slick. We went over all our sector footage—raft cams and set cams—and we couldn't catch you at anything. Val might think we were wise to you, but damn if we can see what proof he's got!"

"Yeah," she smiled and took another sip. "Do you guys ever miss it?"

"Miss what?"

"Miss rafting. I mean real rafting, high-speed—not just porking around in the air like a couple of cops."

"Ooooo," Trek crooned. "You really know how to hurt a guy!"

"Lemme be a little plainer. You're not tied to Panoply. Aces like you could raft for any studio you wanted—write your own ticket."

"Oh Devlin! You're givin me a woodie with all this sweet talk," Lance teased.

"Well then see what this does for you: I walked off that set with mucho clacks, and I'd be happy to pay you boys a mil apiece to help me steal something."

The pair of them grinned at each other.

"Well," squeaked Lance, holding in another toke, "there's no harm in talking it over."

"OK. Do you guys know Mazy and Ming?"

. . .

**At the same** moment, the two young women in question were lying by their own pool—both deck and pool perhaps a little smaller than Trek and Lance's. Mazy and Ming were payraft pilots, and though similarly housed in the Hollywood Hills, they were situated just a bit farther downslope.

Mazy told Ming, "I'm not saying we should agree with her. I'm just saying we ought to go see her and listen to her."

"I'm not gonna talk to that bitch," snapped Ming. When she was all tightened up like this with anger, her lean little form always seemed smaller. From her partner's tension, Mazy saw that a fight was inevitable between them. She sighed.

"I'm sorry, hon, but you're really being immature." Mazy was twenty-two, and Ming nineteen. Being the younger, Ming's identity was a very Big Deal in their relationship. And being the less experienced lover only intensified her insistence on her separate self. Mazy saw she was going to have to talk fast to be heard at all.

"It's because I love you that I have to say this: You're mad at her because—even renegade—Sandy Devlin's still the best rafter god ever made. Come on, Ming! We should never get mad at the best for their gifts. Never get mad at talent—learn from it!"

"I'll respect anyone who respects me! I don't give a shit what they can do otherwise!" Ming's silver hair trembled. She was going shag, letting her pineapple grow out because Mazy was keeping her own.

"Honey," said Mazy. "She's never reprimanded anyone who didn't fuck up, and she comes right out and tells you whenever you do a bitchin job!"

"Oh I do bitchin work—I'm as good as you or her. Better."

"I said 'you' meaning anyone, you silly bitch." Mazy said this laughing, because 'silly bitch' was among their love-words. But Ming could always choose to be offended when her mood so inclined, and now she jumped to her feet. "You talk to her if you want. I'm not gonna."

She jumped in the pool—an unintentionally comic gesture, because the pool was maybe five strokes long, but she started swimming the dinky laps it allowed, getting more steamed each time she had to throw a turn.

"You know what I'm saying, Ming!" Ming's strokes grew noisier, and Mazy half-shouted to be heard. "Sandy Devlin got out! She got out rich!"

She let that sink in.

After three more stubborn laps, Ming vaulted out, dripping, and sat with her feet in the water, glowering and at first refusing to speak.

Mazy smiled a little sadly. She knew it wasn't the word "rich" that had gotten through to her intense partner. It was the word "out." The few times that Sandy Devlin had dressed Ming down had been for reckless risks of rafts and extras. And Mazy knew—as she thought Devlin must have known—that Ming's reckless dives and razor-sharp swoops were the girl's way of dealing with her revulsion at being a rafter at all and the mass murder of which she was part.

**Late the same** afternoon, the five of them were at the young men's place. The grill was still smoking—Sandy had insisted they all eat something before tonight's work. Ming had said, "Screw that, Devlin. I didn't come up here for lunch. Whaddaya want from us?"

And Devlin had handed each of them a neat packet of bills. "Ten K apiece, a small advance. Eat, listen, then walk if you want and keep the clacks."

They'd eaten—all of them except Ming—and now they were waiting to listen, watching Sandy as she paced the deck.

"You know, guys," she said, "I walked off of *Hunger* with six mil in payout cash. I was thinking to give you a mil each to slip into Panoply with me, into the hangar, and help me steal the four fast-rafts off one of the sector boats there."

"Yeah, right," Ming muttered.

But Trek had caught Sandy's musing tone. "You were thinking. But instead?"

"I was thinking too small. Instead we're gonna steal the whole fucking sector boat. I'll pay you a quarter mil each. After the shoot, Sunrise will keep the fast-rafts, but you guys can sell the sector boat on the black market and split the take."

"Whoa!" said Trek. "Bitchin! You really talkin something besides shit now, girl!"

The others were silent, but their silence had a pregnant, ripening quality in which one could almost hear their brains calc-ing out one quarter of the cash a sector boat would fetch on the black market, and the freedom such cash would bring them.

Sandy smiled. "Of course it goes without saying you guys are going to be flying those rafts on the shoot, with machine guns mounted on the bows."

"Of course," grinned Trek and Lance almost simultaneously.

Sandy said, "Just think how it'll feel—I know I am. To be killing APPs, instead of just watching the studio kill extras."

**Near midnight, the** five of them were on-set at Panoply Studios, down in the hangar at the base of the western set wall. All the sector boats—each a great arrowhead-shaped craft with two fast-rafts nested on either side against its under wings—hung from an overhead rack an eighth mile long. The three women helped boost Trek and Lance up onto the boat they'd chosen.

Once the men were aboard, the women stood unspeaking, gazing around at the great concrete cavern. It had a wide, low slot of a mouth that opened directly onto the set's airspace. They advanced to stand in that portal, and view the studio's mighty works.

The shoot of *Quake* was mere weeks away. The set was three-quarters completed and in intensive construction mode. Its whole eastern half was lit. Over there, anti-grav sleds and rafts swarmed in the floodlights. Foam-crete platforms hung athwart the towering girder-frames of high-rises, hosing crete onto their armatures. Smaller rafts closed in like mosquito-clouds on the freshly creted surfaces and sculpted them with little blue-tongued torches. Where they had finished, spray-rigged gondolas converged to tint and texture every surface.

In the nearer, western half of the set there were only scattered zones of activity. One of these was the "crack"—the huge fissure that the quake was to create in the opening scene. Its chasm walls were still being touched up, and here and there shafts of work lights beamed up from its black depths.

Now and again the women turned and looked up to consider the boat they were going to steal. All three of them were fast-rafters, and to their eyes the sector boat looked dangerously big. It was fourteen meters long and nine wide at the tips of its flank-fins. Seen edge-on it looked sleek, tapered like a dirk-blade, but a thick one with those four rafts barnacled to the under-fins, rounded though they were like half-eggs in their nestings. To the women, the sector boat looked as big as a Mack truck.

Lance at last climbed out of it and jumped down. "OK. If we're gonna do this we gotta be real quick about it: as close as possible to zero ticks between our decoupling and our exit from the set. So you guys stand ready, jump in, and strap down the instant we decouple."

Trek decoupled, and the boat dropped like a rock—causing the women neural meltdown, even as Trek switched on his cushion of anti-grav just six inches above the concrete pad. Sandy had to laugh. "You assholes," she said to the grinning Lance.

They swarmed aboard, and the pilots lifted the boat a couple meters for takeoff the instant the women had buckled their harnesses. From her backseat, Sandra Devlin said, "Guys, no offense, truly—but are you sure you don't want me piloting?"

The two young men traded evil grins. Trek turned back to Sandy, his merriment making the little red tufts on his cheekbones sharpen. "You're cargo, Devlin. Buckle tight."

They launched the boat toward the wide low hangar mouth, and—in sheer insolence, it seemed—they flipped the craft on edge, and shot through that narrow sky-slice at right angles to the ground.

They stayed at this full tilt as the big boat whipped out through the enormous set's night air, their left fin-tip just a meter off the street—sped down residential lanes, flying no-lights through the dark. Houses flashed past the eyes of the sideways-hanging women, who with each turn rocked softly in their harnesses. The point of their discomfort dawned on the passengers soon enough: tilted thus, the boat was visible only edge-on to the high raft-traffic busy constructing in the other half of the set.

"Into the Crack!" Lance cackled. "Pucker up, girls!"

"Fuck you!" piped Ming. "I could fly this thing backward and blindfolded!"

Still, the three passengers admitted in their hearts that these two boys were slick at the stick. The women were only seeing the left side of each street they sped down . . . until suddenly, the boat went giddily vertical—still tilted on edge as it did so—and side-hopped something very tall on their blind side, which they only saw below them as they whipped across its crest: the rooftop of the set's luxury hotel with its pool and plantings.

And yawning away beneath them where the next block should have been, there was the Crack, its crooked black abyss dotted with a constellation or two of work lights.

Trek said cheerfully, "Sure hope there's room for us!" as they dropped edge-on like an axe-blade down into the Crack, hitting infra-red as they sank into it.

Seventy meters deep, the opposing walls of ruptured "earth" were still being detailed by techs here and there, and one of these work-zones was not far ahead. The pilots had ramped the boat to eighty klicks. At this speed through the center of the Crack, its uneven walls—narrowing and widening—loomed scarily in-and-out at the passengers.

In the fissure ahead, full-spectrum floods lit scaffolding webbed to one wall, where the little blue arc-torches of creters sculpted the hardened crete, and tinters followed them with their airless tint-rifles. The scaffolds swarmed with at least two-score toiling techs.

Though her lights were still off, as she swooshed past the scaffolding the boat's gloss reflected the wash of the workers' lamps, and the raft gleamed with the deep-sea flash of a big predator swooping very near: the wall thrust in here and clearance from the facing wall was less than nine meters.

Sandy saw in a neat frame of scaffolding a creter's awed face blue-lit on one side by the torch he held, turning just in time to see them sweep near him, big as a house, and three solemn-faced women tilted on their sides watching him as they flashed past.

Fast snaking through more darkness then, the pilots ramping up to a hundred fifty klicks—more darkness, and more dark—and then light and scaffolding again loomed toward them. Coming just past a sharp turn, this onslaught was more sudden than the first, and here there were crete rafts hovering just off the scaffold and cluttering the sector boat's airspace.

Lance and Trek flipped a nose dive and sliced down into deep Crack—and almost made it clear, except for a brief kiss of impact against the boat's upper fin tip, explained an instant later by a glimpse of a raft bottom spinning like a pinwheel away up above them.

Deep they stayed, ramped to a full two hundred klicks, crooking their way through at blur-speed, and then climbing steadily, to erupt up into the moonless night.

They cleared the set wall by less than a meter. The pilots laid the boat back belly-down on the air, and ramped up into the open sky at near four hundred clicks.

"Whoa!" shouted Mazy. "Bitchin ride, boys!"

"Not too bad," piped Ming, pleased in spite of herself. "Little training from us, you guys might become pilots!"

"Ooo, such a little hardcase you are!" grinned Lance. "Just remember what Caesar said: *alea jacta est*!"

"And what's that mean, horn-head?"

"It means the die is cast," said Sandy Devlin. "And so it is."

At Sunrise—just, in fact, as the sun came up—they nested

the boat in a swale in the hills, far enough from the town so the studio spies and electronic eyes most likely would miss it, socketing it in a notch in the slope. Soon they had other hands helping, tarping it over, heaping scythed grass till it looked like a compost pile.

# VII THE VIEW FROM ABOVE

**On his rowing** machine, Val Margolian rivered sweat, reviewing as he oared his recent triumphs and trials.

Pull! *Alien Hunger*: plutonium.

Pull! *Alien Hunger*, Director's Cut, that child of mayhem and mischance: ultra-plutonium.

Pull! He was among the richest men in California.

But. The Cut was such a triumph because it nearly took his life and killed his reputation in one stroke. Through his own folly, the malice of his pilots, and the treachery of Mark Millar, Val had been dragged into the jaws of his own set.

Like some hapless wage slave of the Industrial Era snatched into the mangler that he served, Val had been transformed into a scrambling extra in his own vid, madly fleeing—on camera!—a monster he had himself designed.

His escape from its fangs had killed Raj Valdez, a brave and charismatic action star. Stunned by the mangling that his own opus had given him, Val had retreated to the south of France. His manslaughter moment had been edited out, of course, but he couldn't edit his humiliating performance from his memory.

Until it dawned on him. He'd always been an actor in his every vid, the invisible star that all the others played to. The audience always knew he was there. And if he'd left that moment in the Cut, they would have loved it. The cold killer genius Margolian, caught with his tail in a crack, tossing the male lead to a spider to save his ass.

What tasty schadenfreude his viewers would have sucked from seeing him almost eaten by his art. And as it was, he'd left much in. Had shown his crash (but not its cause), had shown his danger and his near pursuit. A spicy fragment that displayed a great director's willingness to chuckle at himself. And, had captured yet again the whole vid-sucking world's devout attention.

From feeling diminished, Val came to feel enlarged.

His rowing slowed . . . slowed . . . and ceased. He smiled. Now Val Margolian bestrode an even loftier eminence than he had occupied before.

As he showered and dressed, the mirror displayed a man who looked stronger and more handsome than ever. Lean and silver-haired—striking even with that flaw on his face, the crease down his cracked cheekbone, that an idealistic young teacher had suffered in the Zoo long ago.

**Mark Millar sat** his raft above the set of *Quake. Quake:* The Set, he thought. He bleakly scanned his chasm, the little faux city taking shape . . . and thought he might as well just mail this one in.

*Battle of the Somme* had done well at the box office, even very well. That was the problem. In the boardroom they'd say, "*Somme* did very well." A death-knell for his career.

He'd needed a hit to move up next in line as Val's successor. But with so much talent around, directors who did "very well" their first time out were all but doomed to the second-string for life. He'd needed a flick that broke the mold. And a mold-breaker he'd thought Live War would be: extras in armies killing each other—each the other's APPs.

He saw now it was the absence of monsters that had hurt *Somme.* There'd proved to be something repugnant about it: extras forced to kill each other for clacks. It was too like the gladiatorial carnage of Rome, but an industrial scale carnage that left an aftertaste of disgust. People sucked vid to see extras fighting and dying, but *Somme*'s carnage, unleavened by sci-fi demons, made their vile appetite too blatant.

So. He'd ventured into an ugly blind alley with his first. Now, behold his second: *Quake.* Subterranean demons flooding up from the chasm. For all the "crustal movement" that would shake this set, the story was static, flat: cataclysm, demons, turmoil—so standard, after all.

Here came Val in his raft rising toward him. He thought what Val himself had at his mirror: how handsome the man still was. Almost feral his gray eyes, their utter focus. And Mark realized his value to Margolian: he was Val's brightest fan, the one who most completely grasped his genius—the more keenly because he craved but could not hope to match it.

Val docked at his gunnel. "Permission to come aboard, Mark?" He smiled.

Mark put in his handclasp all the warmth he could manage. "Mi raft es su raft, Val." He smiled.

It was but simple truth that his raft was Val's. His mega-success had brought Panoply's Board to heel, and he'd dictated new terms to them, redefining his creative control of every vid that bore the studio's imprimatur. If he chose he could let Mark shoot every frame of *Quake,* then put his own name on it, just like that.

Val would not dream of doing this, of course. Mark was himself doing everything needful to wither his career on the vine. Once *Quake* was released, and he'd added a second minor success to his record, he'd be a second-stringer forever after.

Val took a recliner, and Mark poured them some mocha java. They scanned the swarming set below them. Val gracefully praised it, appreciating touches here and there. Two pros together, talking shop. Mark waited for some show of power from his master, some suggestion to change this or that, but then decided that this visit had a subtler aim—that

Val was simply here to make Mark feel his polite indifference to a project so beneath his greater vision.

He wondered how Val would take the bit of news he had for him. He began weaving his way toward that unwelcome revelation.

"You know, Val," he said, with a hand-sweep below them, "I'm overjoyed, of course, to have all this for my palette. But now it seems the whole wide world is your set."

"Tut, tut, Mark. Just a little piece of the world, no more."

Mark pretended to fish for some clue to where Val would be filming his new vid, the first Live Action to be shot outside a studio. "I just have to say I'm in awe, Val. Wherever it is you're shooting, the logistics must be challenging. . . . I just can't imagine the craft, the command of detail that it must call for."

Val, for his part, pretended not to bite. "You're too kind, Mark, too kind. We are a roadshow I guess, sure enough."

The pending indictment for Murder of an Incorporated Rural Township up in the scenic Trinity Mountains, a township with a high population of ex-extras, was the unacknowledged elephant sitting in the raft with them. Mark dared to push a little harder. "Involuntary extras . . . if I'm guessing right? By god, the leverage that will have on audience response! The fierce partisanship it will awaken in them! The viewers will be rapt."

"Yes. Their sympathy will grip them. They'll feel the great machinery of government that cups them all in its mighty hand." He held Mark's eyes, his smile unfeigned. "Even your own Live War—though it had that beauty of the extras' consensus, the grandeur of their bonding in two armies, couldn't present that unity, that self-sacrifice that will emerge from an actual community under assault."

Mark's nod warmly conceded his greater scope, and somehow in that moment he saw that Val intuited—knew—that Mark had some kind of bad news for him.

Quick as thought, Mark's eyes acknowledged the hunch. "Val," he said somberly, "we've got a sector boat missing from the hangar. A sector boat, and all four of its rafts."

Val gazed at him calmly. "I see. Any defectors?"

"The boat's two pilots, and two payraft pilots, didn't show up for flight-drills today. Here are their names."

Val read, nodding thoughtfully, and looked out over Mark's set—but was actually seeing, Mark knew, complications arising on his own "set" up there in the mountains, and already crunching changes this might mean to his shoot. Mark suddenly remembered how much he loved this man, his invincible artistry. The great Margolian, the Fire-Bringer, the Prometheus of Live Action.

Five anti-gravs stolen, one of them with firepower . . . It had clinched Mark's conviction that Sunrise was Val's target, because only Sandy Devlin—a Sunriser now—could have pulled off such a theft. Devlin. Val's personal demon, his nemesis on the shoot of *Hunger*. She would make good use of her little squadron.

Now Val faced assault on his fleet of cam-rafts. What would he do? Shoot that as well, of course. Record all their counterassaults on his cams. Wasn't that what Val was conceiving right now? Shooting the trapped town's assault on his fleet? A kind of meta-vid!

Not much of a fight that would be, their five boats so hugely outnumbered. No. More likely, the Sunrisers would use them against whatever APPs Val struck them with.

But an exciting notion had begun to tingle through Mark's body. . . .

Val said, "Excuse me a moment," and thumbed his com. "Hello, Harv? I want you to extract from your employee base all the relatives and close friends of the following personnel: pay-boat pilots Mazy Dubois and Ming Slater, and sector-boat pilots Lance and Trek Desmond. Any and all such relatives and friends on our payroll are to be given one year's severance and escorted off the set today. No . . . make it three years' severance." And he returned to his thoughtful gazing over the set.

They both sat silent. Mark was stunned. Val had erred. Just when Mark had thought his mentor above this challenge to his opus, incorporating it, the great Margolian had faltered, and let his anger mar his judgment. Val had sensed it himself—his second-thought revision of the severance terms betrayed the fact.

For by this angry sanction Val had, in one stroke, created an unknown number of new enemies to Panoply. Whatever these people's collusion with the defectors might have been, they'd surely henceforth join his enemies.

Mark's exciting little notion began to grow. He began to think about how he might put a few more rafts into the defectors' hands.

Because more than this—oh what a thrill was starting to steal along the tendrils of his nerves!—more than increasing the Sunrisers' armament, he began to think about launching a groundbreaking shoot of his own.

When Val left, he would com a friend of his, Razz Abdul, a second-string director like himself, over at Argosy Studios.

# VIII
# DEEP SHIT

**Three days after** "the Shootout at the Rasmussen Corral"—it was Japh started to call it that, to keep our spirits up—Sunrise's appeal of the murder charge against it was denied by the state. What need for a meeting? All of us staying for the fight were already busy fortifying our homesteads. Smalls commed everyone the details of the ruling.

We were all individually guilty of homicide, but not just common everyday run-of-the-mill garden-variety homicide. Noooo. This was special circumstances stuff, the slaughter of "Law Enforcement Officers in the Performance of their Duty."

However, though now we were all officially felons, this didn't mean that some of us couldn't keep possession of our land here. Oh no! The state wasn't going to be inhuman about this. It recognized good plot as well as the studio did, and was going to give us "choices" to keep things interesting. After all, not everyone here had pulled the trigger on those tragically misunderstood arresting officers. In fact, we had two options that would let some of us keep living.

Option A: seventy percent of us could voluntarily enter into terms of life imprisonment. Option B: thirty-five percent of us could surrender ourselves for capital punishment.

But this didn't exhaust the state's generosity. There was actually a Third Alternative: no one suffered either penalty, if every one of us vacated Sunrise's acreage, immediately and forever, and all its fifty thousand acres reverted to state ownership.

The state gave us four days to choose A, B, or C. If we didn't . . . well, I loved this part so much, I just have to quote it directly: "Failing acceptance by Sunrise, Inc. of one of the three sentencing options, a correctional force, contracted by the State of California, will inflict capital punishment on the residents of Sunrise Inc., until the requisite percentage thereof have been dispatched."

People howled, they raged and wept, but in the end, most of them got busy. For the next two days the streets swarmed with preparations. Panel trucks and pickups were pulling out in a steady stream for weapon and provision runs down in the valley, some of them bound as far as Bakersfield and L.A. A lot of these vehicles were also carrying the very young or the very old or the very afraid away to safe havens.

Now, with two days down and two to go, Jool was still up at Momma and Auntie's building barricades for their windows and doors, and Gillian was helping her. We were all going to be joining the main fight in town, and were battening down all our homesteads, but no one knew what we were facing. I was with Chops and Japh and we were headed to the Majestic for a gathering of the "effectives"—meaning everyone of fighting age and/or inclination.

As we passed Cap's Hardware we saw our gold-toothed friend out front taping a big hand-lettered sheet to his display window: TAKE WHAT YOU NEED.

"Hold up!" he called, and came down to join us, grinning. "Just like old times, 'ey, Homes?"

"Watchoo mean *Homes*?" Japh said. "You Zoo-meat, we 'Risers!"

"We all Sunrisers now, fool," he laughed.

Cap housed down here in his shop—the man loved being a storekeeper, and loved the town. Here he was living the dream that all Zoo-folk cherished as they scammed and struggled down in their mean streets. It was a full-on, serious hardware store, with a deeper selection of goods than the former owner's, all agreed.

But Cap's personality was also in evidence. He'd installed a modified dentist's chair in one nook where he did tats for his clientele or they could do them on each other. In his display window he'd stationed three female manikins—of the busty hoochie-koochie type—all booted and belted and hard-hatted and jump-suited and hung with so many implements and other butch gear it was a wonder they stayed vertical. There were women in town who didn't know whether to be amused or irked at some sly feminist satire.

"So how are the numbers shaking out?" I asked him.

"Word out from Smalls is it looks like eighty percent stayin' right here for the fight."

Man, that moved us all. It seemed we might field four or five hundred soldiers to protect those less able to fight, but who just wouldn't leave their homes. "Hallelujah," I said.

"Hey," said Cap, "the Studio wouldn't have settled for less meat than that in its grinder."

"So we know it's a studio?"

"Come see Smalls' show, an' you tell me."

The Majestic was full again, and Sandy and Smalls were on the stage when we arrived. Up on the big tattered screen a link from the holo wall was projected—same wall of features in every 'Rise in the state, the morning edition. Smalls had it frozen on its opening frame, some pretty-faced Suit. With all our denim and trail boots and back-holstered shotguns, we looked like ghosts from a bygone era—mountain men watching a vid of the Future.

"First," the sheriff told us, "this is some talkin head from one of the networks, one that's owned—no surprise—by Panoply, which a lot of you've had some dealins with. The man has some beautiful teeth, you gotta give him that."

Sandy spoke up. "People. Before we run it, I just want

to get you to notice the scripting here. He exaggerates the number of extras up here, people from the Zoo that beat the odds, faced death, and won their freedom. He's pitching a big sympathy factor. Meanwhile he questions the state, calls the cops at fault—the whole town is innocent. We're the Good Guys, not just some random population like in all other vids. This whole clip is aimed at building box office."

Smalls started the loop, and the head spoke in a plummy voice. "A mountain town is trapped by the state's mishandling. Sunrise, California, is a beautiful community amid the pines in the Trinity Mountains. Two thirds of the town are retired extras, an irony it would seem, because now fate has scripted them into another dangerous and dramatic dilemma. Four days ago, residents of the town gunned down three of six officers contracted by the State of California to serve a murder warrant on two Sunrise residents. But it appears these residents didn't know these were corp-cops contracted by the state, so inept were the officers in discharging their mission.

"That these residents of Sunrise responded so violently to the would-be arresting officers is perhaps a tragic echo from their pasts, when they fought for their lives on live-action sets. If this is the case, the same violence that won their safety up in this mountain hamlet, now has trapped them in a new and lethal arena of conflict.

"Can anyone be surprised that most of these Sunrisers are now arming to defend themselves against arrest? After all, so many of them have faced death to get where they are, how likely would they be to yield without a fight?"

Smalls stopped the feed. An extra himself, his heavy face was dark with anger. "There's more of the same kinda crap. Now here's the clincher from another prime news slot this morning. You'll notice the shots of Sunrise, like it's practically a preview we got here. My favorite part is where he says he couldn't have written a script like this one. The sonofabitch did write it!"

A close-up of a craggy, handsome face opened the clip. "My name is Val Margolian, of Panoply Studios. I have just learned that the appeal of Sunrise, California, against a charge of corporate homicide of three state police agents has been denied, and a capital sentence pronounced upon the town. I am here to tell you I feel the deepest respect and sympathy for this community."

He continued as an aerial shot of the tree-studded town came on-screen, a traveling shot that slowly scoped our outlying homesteads constellated all over the slopes, our reservoir and its little dam, our new water tower, our old mercury mine, the river in its foaming curves along our southern boundary, the handsome little bridges across that river . . . all this unspooling to Margolian's voice-over:

"A great number of this beautiful community's residents are men and women who bought their citizenship there through work as extras in my own and other studios' live-action videos. My deepest admiration and affection is theirs. How could anyone deny them this respect and admiration? They have won their freedom in these mountains through a baptism of fire, through courage and determination of the rarest kind.

"What tragic ineptitude the state has shown in the serving of a routine warrant! What a cruel irony! We who, in our studios, trade in wild imaginings, could never have written so grim a script as this one! Unsurprisingly, these heroes—against all odds—have declared their will to resist; to fight. Once again they stand at risk of violent death.

"Thus it is that now, we here at Panoply search our hearts and minds for some means to ameliorate this nightmare that has captured the citizens of Sunrise—some way to lighten, compensate the dire hardship they must now unavoidably suffer."

What a mellow voice he had, pouring out this silky shit! It was pure titillation. A tease for the vid-watcher's bloodlust all sugared with pity. "Liable once again to violent death"! It was a sales pitch. There was our beautiful town, like a clip for the vid.

Smalls killed the feed.

"It's pretty plain, folks. Panoply's already got the state contract for execution of our sentence."

Gunfire erupted right outside the theater. It sounded like a shotgun. We all went pouring out into the street.

And there in the middle of it, Iris Meyer sat in her motorized chair, a shocked crowd seething round her. She had a twelve-gauge across her lap, and was rubbing her right shoulder, which apparently the stock of the gun had bruised when she fired it.

People were shouting protests at her, while Ricky Dawes was trying to calm them down. On the pavement in front of them was a bleeding dog, a big black-Lab mix, its torso seriously wounded and its legs pumping. To all the protests around her, Miss Meyer was repeating what sounded like: "It's not a dog, dammit!"

"She's right!" Ricky was shouting. "She's right! Just everyone try ta calm down an' stand back!" Ricky was generally liked and trusted. The uproar dwindled. He asked, "Can I do it, Miz Iris? You already"—an embarrassed little smile here—"bruised yourself."

He put the stock to his shoulder. Racked up a new shell, and shot the dog again very carefully center-mass, making a much bigger wound. The animal's movements were now reduced to just a slight twitching of the paws.

Sheriff pulled a pair of latex gloves from his vest, always particular about keeping his bionic hand clean. He knelt, reached into the wound, and began to spread it.

A long minute passed, quiet enough for those of us nearest to hear the wet little noises his exploration made.

"By God, she's right!" he shouted. "It's hydraulics an' power packs everywhere, feedin a live-skin envelope! The damn thing's bionic!"

I spoke up. "That means two things, people, just like that moss we saw up in our draw. First, something like this . . . it has to be Studio-made! Too expensive to be anything else! And second, if it's Studio, the thing's a walking camera. It's been scoping everything in town for days!"

"It's not just this one," Ricky said. "Miz Iris been seeing strange dogs around town all week. Near a dozen, she says."

A purge started then and there. Iris described six other dogs she was sure were interlopers in town. Four-score and seven rifles were mustered in a blink, and half the town went dog-hunting. I like dogs, and didn't like the idea of shooting them, but in the end I never fired at all because Miss Iris, within fifteen minutes, had spotted three she was sure of, and all three were gunned down. All were opened. All bionic.

But after that, nothing. It dawned on us soon. Why had we got even three? If they were all uplinked to camera feeds, wouldn't all of them have booked once the first one was nailed?

It was like that moss in the draw: we were meant to see, and to be afraid. The Studio was teasing us, building up the tension.

The sheriff passed the word for a reassembly, and as dusk drew down, as many as could fit crowded back into the Majestic.

Sandy Devlin confronted us. "There's a new development, friends. I've been talking to the four new pilots that just brought us our anti-grav Air Force." Some cheering went up here, and she waited to let us enjoy it. "It seems that a lot of people connected to them—directly or indirectly—just got fired from Panoply Studios, and we're already beginning to hear from some of them. It's beginning to look like some inside information about what's in store for us might be had. Because that's what we're facing here, isn't it? We're all going to be in a vid. A live-action vid. And it will sure as shit be Panoply that shoots it."

She let that settle in. Since those vid clips, it came as no surprise to most. "So these firings," she went on, "could mean some luck to us, because what we especially need is information about what kind of APPs we're going to be facing in this vid.

"Now we've got lots of land here, and I think we're all agreed to offer membership in Sunrise for that kind of information—" A mighty roar of confirmation rose from every throat, and Sandy had to wait again till we had all enjoyed that outburst too.

"But some people," she went on, "might just want plain old money for what they know. We're pretty good for cash—especially those of us who're ex-extras or ex-studio—and let's face it, it may be our presence here that's made Margolian bring his little roadshow to Sunrise. We'll put up all we can, but the more you all contribute, the better."

And this suggestion too received a shout of assent, though perhaps not quite so wild as the first.

# IX
# WE LIKE HOW YOU FORK A BIKE

**The next morning,** Panoply went global with the news. A grave Margolian told the world that his studio had accepted from the State of California the Contract of Execution upon the "tragically condemned" community of Sunrise, Inc.

"We pray that its population will yet accept the option of abandoning their homes, heartbreaking though such a choice must seem. But the independent spirit of this community makes this as unlikely as their surrender to incarceration.

"Thus Panoply has undertaken the grim duty of their sentence's enforcement. Compassion for them is our motive, to render them some compensation for their sufferings. Not least of these will be the fact that their ordeal will not go unwitnessed. No. What they endure, and the war they wage against it, will be seen by the world.

"Moreover, for each of our Anti-Personnel Properties they destroy, they will receive the highest kill-bonus ever dispensed by any studio.

"We are pleased to inform Sunrise that it will have additional time for its preparations. The difficulties of deploying a camera fleet for an out-of-studio shoot are new to us, and we cannot be precise. Sunrise will have at least four, and up to seven days from now, before we come to execute their sentence."

Already aswarm with preparations, Sunrise spared no time mulling over the ambiguity of "up to seven days." The last of its evacuees were being convoyed down from the mountains to refuges in the Central Valley. On every block, saws shrilled and hammers knocked, battening-down while steady streams of weapons and matériel flowed in.

Bars were installed over ground-level windows and shielded gun emplacements built on rooftops. In the industrial fringe, the lumber-mills, machine shops, and garages echoed with activity. Every kind of vehicle was tuning and arming and armoring for combat.

Half of the bigger garage—Ike's Engine Repair—was allotted to the SAF (Sunrise Air Force) to hangar its rafts. Unhoused, their engines proved to be of a new generation, their cooling systems' pipes of a new alloy that didn't permit grafting on ice-cannon.

"We have to forget it," said Sandy. "Built-in firepower would be a plus, but we'll just have to carry weapons aboard. Machine guns would be perfect, if only we could find some. I'll tell Smalls to get on that. Meantime, we should all get airborne, work out our battle zones and tactics. Lance and Trek co-fly the big boat. Me, Luce, Mazy, and Radner fly the fast-boats. Ming, you're backup."

Ming stood up, face blazing. "That's bullshit! I'm a pilot! Radner's just a copilot!"

"He co-ed for me my last year at work because he wanted to learn from me, but he piloted five years before that."

"Just listen, Captain Devlin." Ming struggled for calm. Devlin was the best anywhere, but if anyone else had the right to pilot one of these things in the fight, it was Ming herself. "I'm talking no offense to Radner here—Radner, you know that right? I'm just talking straight truth here—I'm faster and more accurate at the stick than you."

The small, wiry Radner, a mild-spoken man in the main, was stung. "You're as fast and as accurate. But truth told, your brain overheats. You get pissed and go wild!"

Sandy said, "Ming. We all know you're a gifted pilot, but Radner's right."

"OK." Her voice was cool but her anger was visible as a slight contraction of her whole body. "Your call. Here's mine. I'm off this crew. I'm fighting somewhere else."

Mazy had sensed Ming's decision before she spoke it. Hearing the ice in her anger, Mazy did not even try to call her back. Watching her storm off, she sent up a mute prayer that whatever part of the fight Ming chose would bring her no harm.

And a half hour after Ming's furious exit, Turp and Frieda Rasmussen, two of Elmer's grandchildren, came tumbling into the shop. The tall skinny girl stridently announced—apparently in a race with her younger, more tongue-tied brother to get it all out first—"We were up by the water tank an' you better get a raft up there quick cause there's four *more* a these little rafts like these ones here parked up there on top!!!" The boy hadn't even pried his lips apart before his big sister was done.

"On top of the water tank?" Sandy Devlin asked.

"That's right, ma'am!"

Trek, eyes wide and his hair-horn seeming almost in erection, said, "What? Are you shitting us, kid?"

"Nossir!" This from the boy, who'd at last found his tongue.

"God damn," grinned Sandy. "Mark Millar, or I'm a fool."

And Mazy saw that if the windfall proved true, Ming could be piloting a raft after all. That they would be together in the air, where Mazy might protect her. And then knew better. Whatever part of the fight Ming found for herself, she was going to stick to out of rage at Sandy.

**Ming marched around** Sunrise's streets. Her anger was so perfect it was a kind of calm. She didn't know what she would do, but she was going to do something. Up and down she marched, looking around at everything, and detesting everything she saw. Born and grown in L.A., she hated this sparkly mountain air—it made all the colors too bright, the sky infuriatingly blue, a god-damned calendar photo. And all these goddamn hicks up here!

A throaty growl started low and grew louder behind her. She turned to see a skinny kid with white hair cruise past riding a chopped Hog. With instant decision, she took off jogging in pursuit of him, right down the middle of town on swarming Glacier Avenue.

Jogged right down out of town and toward the bridge over the Sunrise River, Sunrise's southern boundary. There she found—besides the skinny white-haired kid—Wheel Right Hogs with two other men in its big shed, amid dismembered bikes and a jungle of parts, where the boy was messing with his Harley's engine. Straightening to her full height, she looked at each and announced, "Hi. I'm Ming. I want one of those."

The bear-shaped one had a dense beard in whose foliage only his fat nose, little bear's eyes, and plump lips were discernible. He said, "Well, hello, you pretty thing. I'm Abel. Pleased to meet you too! You say you want a great big hog? A tiny little sugar-stick like you?"

"Hog's heavy," said Cherokee, the taller, leaner one, not unkindly.

Ming's jaw hardened. "Guys. Lemme introduce myself properly. I'm a gay bitch raft pilot. I'm the best fucking anti-graver ever flew. And if you think riding one of those two-wheel fart machines of yours would be a problem for me, then—all due respect—you're as dumb as you look."

Christy, the skinny kid, burst out laughing, and Abel followed suit—a hoarse laugh like a sea lion's bark. Even Cherokee, whose normal style was a Native American deadpan, let out a bark.

"Well, I gotta say," Abel told her. "I like your 'tude, but what kinda clacks you got to spend? This ride here, for instance, is my particular baby."

"I won't buy till I try. You gotta let me check it out."

An hour later, Christy was out on the highway in front of the shop teaching Ming to pop a wheelie. Ming already just about had it down. Watching with satisfaction, Abel said to Cherokee, "Shit! We could teach her to ride that thing straight up a tree!"

They walked out onto the road. "Hold up a second! We gotta talk!" The bikes circled round to them and the four converged, Christy and Ming still in their saddles. "You've got talent," Abel told her. "We like how you fork a bike, sure enough. The question is, can you shoot? Can you one-arm a shotgun while you ride? Cause if you can, and you're gonna stay and fight, we're givin you that hog. And from here on out it's one for all, girl, and all for one."

**Mark Millar and** Razz Abdul lay at their ease in the great tub, passing a little Trinity County weed back and forth as they watched a replay of Val Margolian's vid-cast.

Smiling thoughtfully, Mark said, "He's a true genius,

Razz. It galls you, doesn't it? His gift. Sly old dog! He touched every string of audience empathy. The world market's drooling before he's even shot a frame."

Razz grinned agreement. A tall, taut man, very black, he had a lathed face with cheekbones cut sharp. His status at Argosy Studios as a second-tier director was like Mark's at Panoply.

They were relaxing at Desert Hot Springs in a mineral mud bath. Planning. With both their bodies holstered in the same hot muck, the same conspiracy, their minds meshed easily on all the details. Razz's studio would be the source for half the pilots and rafts, while Mark would supply the other half.

They both loved the opening scene they'd planned: The lieutenant governor is in his chambers, solemnly listening to Margolian. As he listens, there's a fast close-up of a safe beneath his desk, half ajar, with stacks of cash just hastily tucked in it.

Razz said, "OK then. We got a perfect set for the Loot Gov's chambers, got just the guy for Val's part, almost a ringer. But I gotta ask: we sure we want Val giving the loot his orders? Chomp the tail of the dragon? "

"Absolutely." Mark had to hold back laughter as he went on. "You know, I've learned that if you don't commit yourself a hundred and ten percent to a work of art, it will crash in flames."

They both broke up. "I got just the guy—a dead ringer for Val—all he needs is the face scar." More laughter, and another toke.

"Nuts and bolts," Razz said. "There's still a snag on the high-alt boosters for our rafts. Company agrees to our rate but wants us to buy a mandatory month's lease. Real costly."

". . . Options?"

Razz grinned. "I happen to know someone porking the contractor's wife might help us out, with some under-the-table extra for the contractor."

The high-alt rafts were essential to give them the scope to catch all Margolian's lower-alt shoot of (the title was out now) *Assault on Sunrise.* A silence fell between them, a kind of wonder that beset them now and then in their deliberations.

They were doing a new thing in the annals of cinema—capturing Live Action itself and the whole grand, brutal mechanism that it was, Panoply's flotilla like an aerial ant-swarm gobbling the images of the life-and-death turmoil beneath them. And right below the flotilla, that turmoil itself, the floor of it all—the fighting and dying, the frantic improvisations of people struggling for their lives.

Like a living thing, their script had grown, full of cool enhancements of reality. They'd written a scene where the lieutenant gov handed the warrants across to the six goons standing at parade-rest before his desk, warning them to conceal their official identity from the "trigger happy" yokels and to draw their weapons at the least resistance.

As for the scene of these same goons shooting it out with the Rasmussens, they'd moved it from the Rasmussen homestead to a saloon in town. There would be a roomful of hillbilly hardcases drinking alongside the Rasmussens, all armed. The goons would walk in and open their shirts, revealing their sidearms. A gorgeous scene, they'd grinningly agreed—classic Old West, which never went out of fashion.

Mark looked at Razz with a little smile. "I know, partner. There's still that . . . misgiving."

Razz smiled too, more tentatively, waiting for the rest.

"That fear that this exposé of Live Action's . . . inhumanity will close every studio door to us, *saeculae saeculorum*."

Razz smiled a little more. "You can't help thinking about it now and then."

"Well," said Mark, "we just have to think back on Val shooting his first Live-Death vid. The sheer nerve of it. The raw power of Live Action as a genre to capture anything, including itself, will enthrall the world—sweep through Global Audience like a tsunami! The studios won't shut us out. We will own the fucking studios."

"Hey," said Razz. "We're on the same page. Balls out, my brother. Balls out!" And they laughed, like two kids with a brand-new death ray.

# MUCH DEEPER SHIT

**"Let's face it,"** I told them. "It's gotta be me. I'm the fastest one here."

"Bullshit!" Japh wasn't about to let me walk point. But though he was fast, he was lying about being faster than I was and everyone knew it. His size slowed him down. There were about a hundred-fifty of us at a closed meeting, all the most in-shape troops Sunrise had, and their silence was unanimous: I should walk point.

Smalls paced, swept his hand back over his scalp to smooth down the hair he no longer had, scratching his bionic arm.

"All right, it's set. Curtis at point, the first of five gunners. You ten stringers work your way down behind 'em. Any more'n fifteen in the deep shaft is too tight. And—my call as your sheriff—all those fifteen goin deep have to be men."

A high-pitched roar of protest from the audience. Smalls weathered it, arms high for silence. "It's my job to call it, an' it stands. No offense meant to you females in the room, it's just mechanics. We need longer, stronger legs down there. Footing in the deep, steepest parts is gonna be—excuse me—a bitch!"

Some of the women laughed, and most of the men took care not to join in. So. We fifteen were the deep dynamiters and I was point. Thirty feeders and stringers would come down behind us to the edge of the drop-off. Sixty others stringing the upper and branch shafts, and the rest guarding the mine-mouth with Smalls and Elmer Rasmussen, who'd worked in the mine as a young man and had given us its layout.

It was after five when a fleet of pickups and smaller rides brought us two miles up in the hills to the cinnabar mine. We offloaded three thousand yards of wire and beaucoup dynamite.

The whole expedition was the result of a call that Lance had gotten last night. He had a cousin, a woman named Spark—another rafter for Panoply, laid off after his own defection. He told her she had a place up in Sunrise if she wanted it.

"I've got other plans, Lance, but word's out you guys

have cash for studio scuttlebutt on Val's next. I just don't know if what I've got's worth anything."

"Whatever you got's worth a hundred K, and mucho more if it pans out."

"OK then. A friend told me that for a little while during development, Margolian had a working title for his vid. It was Maw, em ay double-you, of Mercury."

Lance could make nothing of it. "OK Spark, you can be sure we'll all chew that over."

"Maw of Mercury" meant nothing to his pal Trek either, but at the morning defense meeting, when he'd aired the tip, Ricky Dawes said, "Mercury. We got the old cinnabar mine. . . ."

It took an ex-extra to grasp it first. My Jool snapped to it. "Think about it! Think of it, like, cinematically! Maw, like a throat. The APPs come crawling up out of the old mine shaft!—rushing up through all those crooked tunnels. Remember what's happening here is a vid—that's how they see it, all spooky angles and atmosphere."

In the after-silence, you could feel it click for everyone in the room.

Now here we all were. It was late in the second day of Panoply's "four-to-seven" and we all felt the clock ticking. We took crowbars to the wooden barricade that had sealed the shaft's mouth for forty years.

"Look here!" someone shouted. "New nails!"

We found a lot more of them—bright sixteen-penny spikes—by the time we'd torn it all down. Someone had been inside before us, and not long ago. A poisonous air breathed out of the shaft mouth.

Everyone got busy. Night would fall on our work underground, but down there night would make no difference. . . .

All fifteen of us put on headlamps. Ten of us carried pouches filled with five-stick clusters of dynamite and coils of wire. Four of us were gunners walking point to sweep the shaft all the way to the bottom for APPs—me, Japh, Ricky Dawes, and Chops, all carrying one sawed-off pump twelve-gauge at port arms, and a second one holstered down our backs.

We switched on our lamps, pulled up our masks, and stepped down in. Stepped down, and down, the daylight shrinking behind us with every step . . . and suddenly I was as scared of using my shotgun as I was of anything I might have to use it on.

Shock waves and cave-ins. Double-ought ricochets. Here, our world was a tube of raw rock and old beams. What was I doing, bringing a firearm down here? These timbers were propping up a mountain over our heads!

The cart rails had been stripped out, leaving just the cross-ties, and they were like a crazy, uneven staircase we stepped down. Our ten stringers kept pace behind us—their work to start down at the shaft's deeper pitch. Please-god that our work wouldn't start at all, that no gun need fire so far underground.

Climbing, your legs are taking you somewhere they want to get to. Going deep like this, their every step is taking you somewhere you want to get out of—a tomb. I'd never realized till this moment how wonderful it feels to have nothing but the sky on top of you.

Our dynamiters unlimbered their loads and started stringing the shaft. We shotgunners continued down, hearing their low voices growing dimmer above us, hearing them thin and reverb out of shape . . . how far down did this fucking thing go? Soon their voices sounded like rumors of restless dreams.

I glanced at my companions. With our masks and jutting weapons and the flood of our weird light around us, we looked like invading aliens—a troop of strangely beaked monsters, edging down into the earth's grip. The air in this long coffin felt silky and dense. The sky seemed like an ancient memory. In our bubble of light, the beams of tarred wood looked like the ribs of a whale that had swallowed us.

Now, the last and steepest stretch: here the miners had made a last sharp dive for the vein as it petered out. Between the timbers, the shaft walls were crumbling. We had to step over drifts of slumped earth as we edged down the trickier pitch—the planet closing back in on its old wound.

And here, the blank wall of earth. The tunnel's end.

"No chance that we passed it?" Ricky asked. "You said it was like a . . . mimic."

"It's possible," I answered. "But somehow I think it's here right at the bottom." Because I saw it the way Jool imagined it: the cameras on the APPs would be filming their whole long, twisty, spooky ascent up the shaft, prime footage of the infernal monsters' rise up through the earth. . . .

We aimed our headlamps on the floor, the roof, the walls. Rock and dirt.

For an instant it hit me as wildly funny. We were like a bunch of archeologists in a cartoon on a dead-end dig. Five baffled folks in bug-masks, no Tut's Tomb in sight. A somber group, all scanning a perfect dead end.

I called up-shaft.

"Nothing visible. I guess we just blow it, be on the safe side."

"Wait," said Japh. "Turn your head back the way you just turned it—slow now."

And as I faced again up-shaft, I saw it too. A hint of a regular pattern in the chopped stone directly over our heads as my beam swept it. There were—here, there . . . everywhere—little rounded nodes nested among the crude planes of the broken rock.

"You see them?" Japh asked.

"Shit!" Chops hissed. "The rock's full of 'em!"

We beamed them at close range: smooth tapered hemispheres, about the size of a fist. They looked like the narrow ends of big eggs.

"String it faster guys!" Japh called.

"Stop," said Ricky. "Turn your light away from the wall."

When we put the wall back into shadow, we realized that it had started glowing softly here and there. Each one of the nodes was showing a faint blue luminescence of its own.

"Were they doing that before?" asked Chops, the answer in his voice.

"We would've seen it," I said. What now? I called up-shaft. "Fuck stringing it! Spool the rest down here and get it wired. Fast!"

They came down in a little landslide of boots and dirt. All fifteen of us now in this last few yards of the shaft, working away, our noise-level low but still sounding to me like a riot down in that tubular grave.

We weren't a minute into it when we heard a sharp little splinter of sound. Like cracking rock, I thought.

"They're working free!" said Japh. And we saw the nodes swell, then contract, then swell again larger than before. Again that sound of crackling rock. You could see fissures sprouting through the stone around them.

"I think you better hurry it up," I yelled to the dynamiters. "String and fuse and drop it! We'll blow it where it lies!"

Stone snapped like pistol shot. Several of the dynamiters bellowed almost simultaneously: "LET'S GO! TAKE OFF! GET THE FUCK OUTTA HERE!"

And I saw all the nodes like a constellation seem to focus. Like one big compound eye comprehending us all.

The fifteen of us launched ourselves upslope as one, fifteen pairs of male legs now demonstrating their superior endowments of stride-length and driving force. The echoes of our feet sounded like a stampede, like something was chasing us up from the bowels of the earth.

Up the steep stretch, then pumping wildly we climbed the easier grade. I kept glancing back, throwing my beam behind us, but nothing was following, not yet . . . . How long did they need to switch fully on? How fast were they?

The upper shaft guys had finished—they were running ahead of us. We neared the mouths of the branch tunnels, saw those crews pouring out too. All of us running now, running for the high, far mouth of the mine, and—now visible—the star-hung night sky.

I was last out. Before I had quite reached the shaft mouth—not quite in the clear but too scared to wait any longer—I screeched, "BLOW IT!"

And was so instantly obeyed that the whole sky seemed to collapse around my ears, and a hurricane of dust sprayed my back as I leapt out into the open air, and when my feet touched earth again, it was like landing on a gigantic trampoline, the blast's convulsion of the mountainside launching me into a longer and higher arc through the air.

I lay there, seriously bruised in the dusty grass, as the aftershocks kept rocking me. The whole branching shaft groaned and settled, the mountain shuddered and repossessed the void dug out of it so long ago.

# THE CHOOSERS OF THE SLAIN

**Wagner's "Ride of** the Valkyries" trumpeted in Val Margolian's headset as he lay in his recliner, watching a fleet of helicopters slicing the sky above the jungles of Vietnam. A classic vid. Solace in it as his mind's eye superimposed a scene of his own: a fleet of anti-gravs filling the sky above Sunrise, bringing its doom in silent flight like Angels of Death. As he tapped time to the music, he counted off his recent sins, accusing himself for his fingers' faltering on the keyboard of Art.

The first sin, arrogance. He knew—as a Bach knows

each note of his fugue—just the keystrokes where pride had made him falter.

*From The Maw Of Mercury* had been his working title for *Assault On Sunrise.* Some echo of it had reached its prey, and warned them to look in the mine.

Even to have a working title was callow excess, but to put such a clue in it—as if he couldn't help tipping his hand, like an amateur! Word always gets out in a studio, especially with a vid so deep under wraps. How could he have been so stupid?

The fatal words were a signpost to his opening, a beautiful sequence that now he would never shoot. So clear still in his mind's eye, that visual fugue of menace and swift movement.

Its POV would have been entirely that of his APPs, all of them socketed in stone, nested in the gloom of their own faint light. They would hatch from the rock, split and shed the stone as their bodies sprouted into shape and their wings broke free.

Then—their bodies still their only light—they would have flown up through the crooked shafts, a Stygian armada. Past ancient timbers and cross-ties like ladders to the sky, till from the mine's mouth, they erupted up into the rising sun.

Airborne then, the blur of their wings like burnished copper, his children would have knifed the sky, their sabers flashing, their whirlwind descending on the town. . . .

That whole gorgeous sequence obliterated! Two hundred of his Black Death Angels, snuffed out by the collapse of the cinnabar mine.

It wasn't a crippling blow. Not that. But it made him uneasy to be now so short on reserves.

No matter. He must let it go. Just this morning he'd learned that his shoot faced a new threat, or at least a dangerous distraction. . . .

He punched replay. Again the cloud-striding music, brazen, triumphal chords that lofted the Hueys across that plain of palms. Their blades were rotary scythes for reaping whole jungles of souls.

He was Valkyrie too, of course, his rafts and his cunning APPs choosers of the slain. But he was not at heart a death-dealer. He was first a storyteller, an artist impassioned by narrative. He followed truth down its own dark alleys, and as he'd followed those alleys down, death had shown itself to him as truth's key ingredient in this day and age.

He watched Coppola's killers crossing the sky on wings of Wagner. Canting his head at a thoughtful angle, touching the crooked crevice of his cheekbone, Val weighed himself . . . and his heart said, so be it. What else could he do but proceed? And where else on the planet could a man find a more wonderful job? To rule the Earth from the skies, to call its wars into being, its tragedies and victories . . . ?

But how, how could he have played such a fool? For his sin of pride, his working title had not been enough. No. Next came the sin of anger. To have petulantly expelled the raft thieves' blameless friends from the studio! This had published the title that his pride had coined. All his layoffs had brought to Sunrise reports of every hint they'd heard.

Anger, his nemesis. Anger, his blind side. It always flared

up in you just when you were least ready to outthink it! Well then. The work was wounded, no helping that. But its brilliance, its beauty were intact. The drama—a dynamite-factory of a drama. All those people so well armed, so schooled to weaponry. What a troop of guaranteed fighters, and all defending each other instead of just themselves. He still held a gem in his hands, and he meant to cut it flawlessly.

Audrey commed, one of his chiefs of APP Testing. "We're ready, Val."

"Great, Aud. Send me a boat."

As he rafted across the burgeoning set of *Quake,* he conceded that Mark Millar had an eye for layout. But how would he do in the field, on unknown ground? Mark's greatest talent was in assisting Val's own work. Perhaps as a parasite on that work he'd do equally well.

He joined Audrey and her crew down in APP testing's amphitheater beneath the set. Pilots practiced APP evasion here, in case they should be downed on-shoot, but the subject of this test wasn't going to be doing any evasion.

Clearly, the man who lay on the gurney was incapable of evading anything—an older man, hair half white, whose Irish-featured face was contorted by paralysis on one side, so that he wore a cramped, pained smile, the smile stranger still for the wetness of tears in the orbits of his eyes. He was murmuring into a com, which he clicked off on Val's approach.

"Hey, Mr. M." His words were pretty clear because only a corner of his mouth was frozen. "I'm O.K. 'bout this, no sweat. I was jus' sayin g'bye to m' wife."

"I understand, Mr. MacMahon. May I call you Jack? Please call me Val."

"Sure, Val, and . . . I really 'preciate what you've done for my Shelly."

Two million dollars were secured in his wife's account in return for this gift of what were—at most—the two weeks left of his cancer-riddled life. ". . . But I don' wanna talk. Can't we just?"

"Instantly, Jack. I just have to say how I admire you, how brave and fine this is, what you are doing. There will be no pain at all, and death will be instantaneous. May we blindfold you?"

"Sure . . . I'd 'preciate that."

Standing so near this disease-dwindled shape in a hospital tunic suddenly gave Val himself a sense of nakedness, the sensation he'd felt on the set of *Alien Hunger,* running for his life with an arachnid APP tight on his ass. An ice-cold emptiness between the skin on his back and the out-thrusting fangs. He'd reached out to pat the man's shoulder, and this flashback froze his hand in midair. Catching himself, he converted the gesture to a go-ahead signal to Audrey, and stepped back from the gurney.

The APP was released into the amphitheater the moment the blindfold was placed. And as far as anyone could tell, all Jack MacMahon knew of it was a sudden soft yet powerful hum, a stirring of the air, and a touch, no more. Then he lay perfectly still.

Val asked, "How long are we looking at, Audrey?"

She smiled, a dark lean woman with probing eyes. "There's a fifteen minute minimum. But it's lunchtime—want us to make it an hour so you can grab a bite in the canteen?"

Val turned his gaze, his half-smiling surprise, full on his employee. "Ouch! Is that your way of saying I'm a monster? Understand—I'm not offended. You're tops at your job here, and it's yours as long as you want it. But really—shouldn't you quit? Feeling that way?"

"Not if you don't insist I do, Val." She smiled cooly. "I like to smartass about people's morals because I don't have any."

Val chuckled. "There are those who preach morals, and the rest of us who have work to do in the real world. Let's go for the quarter hour." A grin here. "I'll skip lunch, and settle for taking a leak."

And he strolled out of the arena to the showers. In the bathroom, he took time to look in the mirror a while. He liked the new calm he saw there. Audrey's attitude had helped, had centered him.

Was this fellow in the glass here a monster? Sure. A monster-maker who was about to inflict his homicidal brood on people who had not volunteered to face them.

"And how do you feel about that, Mr. Margolian?" he asked himself pleasantly, seeing the glint of his own genuine curiosity in the question.

"I feel . . . airborne. I feel I am about to witness a miracle of my own creating." He studied the face that had just said that, and saw there a calm man who was the destiny, the doom of several thousand people. Who was a Valkyrie, a chooser-of-the-slain.

And, smiling slightly, he said, "So be it."

He returned to the arena with a minute to spare. Stood chatting politely with the techs who were waiting to paralyze what emerged from Mr. MacMahon's body. Soon enough came the powerful rupturing of meat and bone. Val scrutinized what emerged. Very satisfactory . . .

**Val did go** up to the canteen then. Carried some coffee to a secluded table. Satisfied with the predators of *Assault on Sunrise,* he returned his thoughts to the predators who meant to prey on him.

For the past few days, his studio spies had been filing some very suggestive reports: a movement of shoot hardware over at Argosy Studios, some funny business with raft inventories at Val's own Properties Division, and several discreet meetings between his own Mark Millar and Argosy's Razz Abdul.

At first Val thought this was a cat's-away romp between the two wannabes. A case of some juniors going extracurricular while the master was up in the mountains.

Until it occurred to him to wonder whether the pair's Work in Progress might not have his own shoot in Sunrise for its subject.

Then he'd considered those blue mountain skies from a new perspective, and how his own bright flotilla of shootrafts would look, maneuvering in that brilliant sky above the embattled town. . . .

To weigh the prospect of this spectacle was to be enraptured by it. He recognized at once that the younger men's aim had to be the theft of his own shoot, because of the incredible scenes that shoot would yield, captured from overhead.

More focused researches clinched it. Razz Abdul had signed off a major work order with FLOSS-WERKEN: the installation of high-altitude augments on the anti-grav engines of an impressive little fleet of rafts.

There it was. They could only need a high-alt fleet because they were going to shoot his shoot from above.

For the first time he found that he actually liked Mark Millar, his vision and daring. What footage there! The extras beseiged by APPS down in their town, and above them Val's flashing fleet lit first by the sun and later by the moon, and above them Mark's boats filming it all!

It opened Val's directorial third eye right up. The two second-stringers had found a cinematic mother lode. Val's own pioneering use of public airspace in this vid—real-life Live Action—had laid his shoot naked to their cams.

If they kept their heads, the pair of them were on the brink of an epochal vid—a genre-spawner.

There he himself would be for them, down in the aerial traffic above the town, and below him the human/alien seethe of combat on the rooftops and in the streets. How neatly he'd been surrounded. Imprisoned in his work, while they gobbled his vid, picked his cinematic carcass to the bones.

He commed the capo of his legal eagles.

"Zachary? Val."

"Hi, Chief."

"Zack, I want everything on the Studio's proprietary statutes. Here's the situation . . ."

After Val commed off, he sat thinking. From feeling under siege, he'd come to feel much better. Worst case, he could freeze their release, force them to share title before he allowed it, and then only after *Sunrise* had hit the screen. Best case, he could own their vid.

Meantime, he could spare the cams to shoot them shooting him. And could he not contrive some guerilla action against them in the bargain? Could he not eke out some APPs for them as well as for his extras? Maybe.

Peacefully absorbed now, Val followed branching trains of thought. His handsome face was perhaps most likeable in moments like these. The man himself was absent from it, and only his conception filled it. He had a look of faint absent wonder, his eyes delighting now in this detail, now in that, his face guileless—except that the crease of his cracked cheekbone (now and again darkened by shadow) gave his look an accent of darker intent, even a faint gleam of homicide.

**Racquetball made such** a wonderful racket. While they played, Razz and Mark's talk was as staccato as their hotly contested game.

"Moonlight! That's gonna be bitchin!"

"Backlight the shoot-rafts against the moon!"

"All silhouettes!"

They swatted logistics back and forth in the echoing

court. They'd shoot from payrafts, these the most agile anti-gravs, and would have a high-alt modification, a major refrigeration unit added for that output.

They'd been of two minds about how much their "pirate" fleet should interact with Margolian's fleet. Mark had been for staying aloof from them, Razz for swooping down to get close-ups of them at work. But now, as they sat in the sauna, Mark conceded. "They're our cast, after all," he said abruptly into the silence. "They're part of our cast, that Panoply crew. You're right. We have to dive to close-ups. Those rafters, after all, will be our heroes and demons."

"Now you're talking. We can get some comedy going! We can swoop down and hang just off their bows, and we can remonstrate, upbraid them—all in fun, right?"

"Exactly! And some straight stuff too! Capture some of their conflict maybe, their doubts."

"You see it now, don't you—I knew you would. Irresistible stuff!"

"Absolutely. And listen: your name goes first. I brook no denial." And, after a beat, Mark added, "From the heart, Homes. Mos def!"

And they both erupted in wild laughter, knowing they had it now, that they were going to get it just right. As long as they had even, worst-case scenario, bootleg footage, they were going to make it into vid history.

# XII
# THE MONSTER'S FLESH

**Ming rode her** Harley into the hills behind Abel and Christy for some battle practice. Cherokee, their motor-magician and official hog-whisperer, was at the shop resurrecting—as only he could do—Abel's Indian, a bellowing dinosaur of a bike that Cherokee openly coveted for his own.

"This look good, guys?" Abel asked them. His ATV towed a two-wheel trailer of empty wooden wine kegs. Below them stretched gentle slopes of hollows and hillocks to give the rolling kegs an erratic pattern.

"Set 'em loose," said Ming.

Abel kicked open the tailgate latch and the kegs started tumbling and jouncing downhill. Gunning their bikes, Ming and Christy zigzagged after them.

They fired their pumps one-armed, the butts to their hips, punching double-ought wads through the little juggernauts' staves, working their slides one-handed. Ming had nailed four by the end of their run.

"Damn!" cried the guilelessly outspoken Christy, a natural enthusiast for all forms of vehicular insanity. "You're a rock star! I taught you biking, you gotta teach me rafting, sis!"

Ming always dealt very crisply and unsentimentally with young Christy—actually they were of an age—but there was something about that "sis" of his that deeply irked her because she found herself liking it.

"Speak of the devil!" Abel crowed as a raft came dropping down, Trek at the helm. He hung its bows down so he sat almost facing them, easy in its slanted bottom.

"I love your work! I been watching you make those barrels dance! Hate to interrupt, but would you guys put off maneuvers an' come to the hangar? Somethin' big's cookin we need your help on."

The "hangar" being Ike's Engine Repair, where the fleet—now nine craft—was housed.

"I'm not flying a raft! No way, no how! I told that bitch that!" Ming surprised herself with this outburst. Had she been arguing mentally with Devlin all along?

Trek raised a placating palm. "No! She thought—we

thought you'd think that. We need you guys to make a run, and it's a run on wheels we need. This is deep-wraps, guys. It's I-shit-you-not life and death. Get Cherokee an' follow me. You're gonna have to leave by dark."

In the back corner of Ike's Engine Repair's big-vaulted garage was a small, crowded machine shop. Devlin bade everyone in. Mazy, Lance, and Radner were already there. Shutting the door, she sealed them all in the cold oily smell of machinery. It was somehow the right scent, a smell of mustered weapons, of danger and urgent defenses.

"Mazy?" Devlin prompted.

Mazy's eyes always had a merry squint to them, like she was wondering if you'd understand a joke she wanted to tell you. She looked at the bikers—a little smile for Ming—and cleared her throat. "We need you to bring something up from the Valley. What we need you to bring us . . . is a sample of what's gonna start killing us when the shoot starts. We just got word of it. Sandy dangled a mil of her own clacks, and we hooked a studio tech." She broke out in a grin. "What we have here is gift-of-god luck. The guy will be in Outer Redding at a bar at sunup.

"The thing is, we do not dare the air. Any of our rafts will draw sharp eyes, not to mention they're stolen and could draw the heat. But bikers, well, they're thick as fleas down in the valley."

"Hey!" protested Abel.

"Will you guys do this?" Mazy asked with a winning smile—which Ming in her heart had to admit that she still found pretty damn winning. They hadn't spoken since she'd joined the bikers. "If you bring it back, we might be able to find out how to kill this fucking shit that's gonna be killing us."

Abel: "Would we do this? Does Howdy Doody have little wooden balls?"

Cherokee: "Is the bear Catholic?"

Christy: "Does the Pope shit in the woods?"

The Wheel Rights answered themselves in a chorus of damn-straights and fuckin-ayes. Sandy Devlin offered a money belt to Abel, and then noting his girth, switched it to Cherokee. "Meeting's set for early tomorrow—it's the safest time to get there. Buckle this five mil on under your leathers. The guy's name is Dukes. He'll be in Outer Redding at the Pink Elephant and he's got a sample of what the APPs on this flick are going to be made of. Nano-gel."

Abel spoke. "You're puttin a shitload of faith in us. We won't fuck it up."

"Famous last words," piped Christy, an automatic comeback of his to any of Abel's more solemn utterances.

**So just before** midnight the bikers roared down through the mountains headed for the Five. The three men liked to ride gaudy when they took their bikes down to the Valley. Christy'd had his Hanger 'kick tanner cure him a road-killed skunk's pelt, and the kid had made this a plume curving over his helmet crest. The open jaws frontal just above his eyes. Portly Abel liked buckskins with major fringes. These roared like soft brown flames off his bulk as he ran at full throttle. Cherokee wore his own totem helmet. He'd found a big red-tail, dead of starvation up in the mountains during a drought year. Her wings—half unfolded—he'd lovingly polyurethaned and mounted, and they swept back from the temples of his WWII infantry helmet. All three had hair enough to banner out from the fringes of their warlike headgear.

Ming scorned Panoply and panache. She wore only big silver reflecting goggles like bug's eyes, above which her short ragged 'do flashed silver as the sun came up. Plain black leather wrapped the rest of her.

The Five was pouring under their wheels as the east grew pale, and Redding hove in sight just after sunup. It sat on low ridges to either side of the freeway. Outer Redding littered some slightly higher hills to the east of the healthy part of town. Up there, tattered trailers perched on bulldozed niches in the slope, and along the Z of bad road climbing that slope larger shapes stood here and there—of cinder block or corrugated metal or rain-bleached carpentry with shingled roofs. Outer Redding. Warren of drug kitchens. Haven of highwaymen. Home to numerous wheeled bandits of the breed who'd attacked Curtis and Jool a year before on their last run down to L.A.

Midway up the slope, the Pink Elephant looked like a gravely decayed bon vivant. Its stuccoed walls had begun pink, and been touched up over the years with whatever shades or near relatives of that color had come to hand, till presently its hue was more like skin disease. It had a whole wall of windows, but half of these were boarded over with plywood thickly hieroglyphed with felt-tipped gibberish and anatomical cartoons. It sported a neon sign on which a few letters of tubular glass still survived: INK EL.

"They were right," grumbled Abel as they kickstanded their rides, cocking an ear to the silence of the place. "This is as good a time as any to come to this shit-hole." He sniffed the air. "You can smell everyone sleepin off their drunks."

The double metal door wore scabs of old posters flaking off of it. It looked like it had been kicked by everything known to man. The four of them entered a wide, rambling interior, irregularly partitioned, that seemed to stretch in all directions into a green gloom.

Here and there bulky men slept with their heads on their arms on the beer-puddled tables. Three jukeboxes of different vintages stood along one wall. The glass on two of these had been caved in.

The Sunrisers filed quietly among the tables, crossing dark floors, with an occasional crunch of glass under their boots. They passed only one conscious patron, a gaunt, pale woman staring at them from a booth she shared with a huge man who snored, his head on the table. His earring—a brass chain—dangled in the puddle of spit his mouth had leaked.

A final turning, and they found him in a dark corner booth, a biggish bald man armed as they were: a chopped twelve-gauge across his back and two cross-holstered forty-fives below his ribs.

"Dukes?" asked Abel pleasantly.

"Just so," the man smiled. They tucked into the booth

and quietly introduced themselves. Perhaps stirred by their entry, groggy bikers were becoming more or less vertical in the gloom, coughing and belching, cracking their first beers of the day.

Dukes was a smiling, rangy man. He looked in his fifties and tough. Between his forearms on the table stood a full pitcher of beer and glasses. He began filling these. Only Ming declined.

Amenities done, Dukes said, "Well then. So show me, please."

Cherokee discreetly unlimbered the belt and handed it under the table. Faint papery sounds rose from Dukes' busy fingers.

He smiled at them all and strapped on the belt under his jacket. Brought something up from his lap, and set it on the table: a lidded one-gallon paint can.

"OK, kiddos," he said in a low voice. "Lean real close. I'm due back this evening. Sorry this has to be quick and dirty, cause you got some risky shit here. This piece of gel is in its base active mode. It's pure raw material and gives you no clue to the shape of the APPs that'll be made of it. This is the stuff in its, like, minimal or rest mode, called PSI: Pursuit, Seizure, and Ingestion. Meaning it'll catch and consume anything organic that moves.

"When you come to trying to work with it, dump it into a walled-in pen or pit with smooth vertical sides and no cracks or seams it can ooze through, OK? Cause if it can, it will. It's highly fluid and can exert powerful pressure. To capture it and put it back in whatever container you're using"—Dukes grinned here—"you'll need your paint stick."

And he pulled out something that looked like a foot-rule, with little nodes on it instead of numbers. "You stick it into the gel and press here and the gel coheres around the stick. You push this node to drop it back in the can. I don't have any idea what-all this stuff can do beyond the basics I'm gonna show you, but just bear in mind your APPs are gonna be made of it. So, come on."

The five of them slipped out through that warren-like gloom as discreetly as they could, and went round to the back of the establishment. Here sprawled a chaotic dump of motor parts and box-springs, chassis and old appliances, and every other kind of bulky trash. The sun—bright gold across the Valley—put the Elephant in chilly shadow. "Over here should work," said Dukes, leading them over to an abandoned claw-foot bathtub.

"You see I found us a guinea pig."

A very sizeable tarantula was in the tub. It was futilely trying to scramble up the slippery enamel sides. The drain hole's plug was firmly in place. "OK," said Dukes. "Watch everything I do."

He popped the lid off the can, and thrust his "paint stick" inside it. He thumbed a node . . . and drew out a translucent sphere, blackish green. This globe just perceptibly rippled, yet gripped the stick as if welded to it. There was a fugitive coruscation within it, blurred constellations slowly cycling. Dukes thumbed again, and the sphere plopped into the tub.

The gel instantly responded to the scrambling spider:

flowed swiftly to it, and engulfed it. Its struggle was in slow motion now, its working legs seeming to smoke at first, and then to become smoke. The bulky abdomen lasted longest, became a cloudy ovoid, became fumes, and then was gone.

"Now look," said Dukes. "Notice that it's just a little bigger?"

"It . . . it's hard to tell," said Ming.

"Trust me. Feeding adds to their mass. Excuse my putting it this way, but the more of you Margolian nails with this shit, the more he'll have."

There was an unmistakable click, the hammer of a firearm right behind them. A gravelly voice said, "Dead easy folks. Perfectly still. Whatever that is, I'm takin it."

"OK man," Dukes said carefully, "I've gotta pick it up with this." He tucked the stick in, the gel englobed around it, and he turned to face their intruder. "Terkle!" he barked with disgust, apparently recognizing this huge goon with big bony shoulders and acromegalic jaws, a long chain earring dangling from his lobe. Given his size, his stealth in coming up behind them was remarkable.

"You asshole, Terkle! There's no way you can use this thing."

"You shittin me? That's some kinda high-tech shit there! Hand it over or I plug you all where you stand." He was holding a machine pistol with a big clip under the stock, and showing them a forty-five caliber muzzle.

"Shit! All right. Hold out the paint can and I'll drop it in."

"Fuck that. One of you hold the can."

Dukes turned to Abel. “Take this, man, and hold it so—” He whipped the globe at Terkle’s face, pressing the stick’s release button. Flattening like a pie on the goon’s face, the gel instantly englobed his whole head. Reflexively he flung away his gun to tear the gel off with both hands, and his hands too were instantly engulfed in it.

“Shit!” said Dukes. “The thing’ll get too big to handle! Grab his fuckin arms and try to pull at least his hands outta there!”

A ghastly tango commenced—two of them on each arm hauled mightily against the galvanic rigidity of the big man’s muscles—and then, suddenly toppling them off balance, the arms came free—handless, with black ragged wrist stumps.

“Hold him up!” Dukes shouted, for Terkle’s legs were buckling and he was going slack. “Hold him up! We can’t let it get to the rest of him, the fuckin gel will get huge.”

They propped the goon and Dukes held his stick poised above the hungry globe as it worked on the head and neck. Terkle’s face bulged huge within the sphere—a drowned man seen through the porthole of a sinking ship. His hands, like two crabs drowning with him, were going smoky.

Dukes thrust in the stick and the gel cohered, obedient—as it were—to the extent that the sphere ate the neck the rest of the way through, and then allowed itself to be lifted free, the skull still dissolving within it. Terkle’s body slumped to the ground.

“Shit!” raged Dukes. “We’ll need at least a three-gallon bucket now! You asshole!” And he kicked Terkle where he sprawled, headless and handless.

Abel and Cherokee searched the trash heap, and came up with a water-cooler, empty. "Can you get it into this?"

"Bring it here." Dukes studied the much larger globe. "OK, he's softened up enough. Hold the jug under it."

He touched the stick differently, and gel began to elongate, tapering downward. Its contents were a smoky skull and almost shapeless hands, and these too elongated and tapered, the skull seeming to make a comical grimace as it narrowed, narrowed down through the bottle neck.

A scrap roll of duct tape yielded them a sealer for the mouth. "Thank you, my friends," said Dukes. "I truly hope you stomp Margolian's ass. Now we should all bid adieu to scenic Redding."

**Dr. Winters, Sunrise's** veterinarian and high school chemistry teacher, selected Trish Meeks as his assistant for testing the nano-gel sample. Trish's style was sort of Hillbilly Goth—purple lipstick, hair half petroleum-black and half screaming-scarlet. She'd been a real wiseass in class two or three years back, but Winters had early on tricked her into admitting how smart she was, and had been employing her ever since.

The doctor was a man who would provide anyone—more or less on request, in his dreamy and bemused way—with concise and informed judgments on everything from fertilizer composition to high-tech hog paint jobs. Not a very demonstrative man himself, he was almost universally liked. Even touchy Trish Meeks—and this at times when she was not actually working for him—used Winters' house key every week or so to let herself in and make sure he had enough of the right things in his fridge and cupboards. Fuck you if you asked her about it, but everybody knew it was so.

As to where they would set up a lab to work on the specimen, Cap came to him with a good idea. When Cap had bought his hardware store, Winters had shared with him countless little wonders of physics relevant to the tools he sold, and of chemistry relating to his paints and varnishes. . . .

Now Cap said, "Look here, Doc. My store shares a concrete foundation wall with the Masonic Building next door. I already cut through it so people can move between the buildings without exposure outside. Give you two ways in and out. Use the Masonic's basement—it's bigger an' emptier than mine, an' we can mount guards on both your entries."

So in the Masonic Building's basement Winters and Trish Meeks installed a lawn pool, a stout metal frame which supported a thick, supple plastic cavity with almost sheer walls. A dozen assistants made shelves, reconnected the plumbing of an old sink, and saw to stringing strong lights everywhere.

At last they cut off the top of the bottle and extracted the gel with the control stick. It was a hefty load lifted one-handed—about the dimensions, when spherical, of a small beach ball. They set it into the pool liner, and keyed its release from the stick.

It sat inactive. Menaced with a rod, its globe surged forth engulfing it, then flowed away and drained entirely off it. It would engulf any object set in motion near it, but, finding it inorganic would eject it.

After a series of such little experiments, Trish lit one of her cigarettes—severely rationed by Winters in the "lab" here—and blew smoke on the gel. Its sphere bulged out a bit to meet the smoke's impact, seeming to taste. "What it looks like, sir," she said respectfully, "is that you can't get anything inside it that it doesn't wanna eat."

"That's right, Trish. Of course, we'll try applying caustic substances topically, to see if it can be damaged that way. But I'm afraid we'll have to start by feeding it, to see if we can learn anything by watching it ingest something."

"Patti's Pets has got some white rats."

# XIII
# ENLISTEES AND PROPERTIES

**Day Three. Panoply** Studios informed Sheriff Smalls of the "Shoot Schedule"—not of its start date, mind you, but of its duration. It would last two days, starting both days at sunrise—nice touch, that—and ending at midnight. There would be three "Acts" each day, separated by "substantial intervals for rest, recuperation, and repair."

Japh and I walked down Glacier Avenue. The town was alive with hammers and saws, people all over from the roofs on down, the street full of traffic. Two rafts dangled iron laddering from cable hooks, laying it for bridges and gangways to join all the rooftops. Inside, jackhammers were connecting basements where possible, following Cap's example. Headlamps and floods were being installed on eaves and gables everywhere, to light things up for the night fights.

As we walked I noticed Japh had picked up Sheriff Smalls' trick, scratching his own prosthetic forearm, a souvenir from *Alien Hunger,* from time to time when he was thinking. Right now he was sorting out what he wanted to say to me.

He said, "Curtis." Being patient. Trying to make me see his side. "Ike Klemm's as smart as George Junior, yes. And he has scads of friends down there. That's cause he's a shoulder-thwacker, hale fellow well met. George Junior makes himself heard, an' they call him an asshole cause he says whatever he thinks, but people listen to him for just that reason. I just trust him more."

My friend was beginning to chap my ass. "Hey. My brother! Listen to yourself. You're talking the Georges here!"

"I know! True! The Georges are batshit. But I trust 'em. You know, all the jokes Ike tells, I don't think I've ever seen him really laugh."

"The only time George laughs is when he's callin you an idiot."

"Yeah, but he's really laughin."

I had to think that one over. And then I had to smile. "You might be right, old tight."

Along the downslope rim of Sunrise, and spreading maybe two miles farther down the hills, were the homesteads of the Hangers, most of them as old as Sunrise's, but outside her corporate border. A neighbor community of generations' standing.

Hangers strictly respected all property lines with Sunrise. Scores of Hangers visited us, shopped, drank, ate out, and partied with us every night of the week.

At the same time, a humorous tension prevailed between our populations. Sunrisers gripped the Hangers' hands or hugged them in greeting, and said, "Hey, Hang, you lookin good for a guy from Creepy Hollow."

Because downslope of Sunrise, though still fertile and verdant, the open ground diminished, and Hangers lived somewhat more closely with their trees, and in their little shaded vales, while Sunrisers lived larger and sunnier. Both groups took pride in their lifestyles, and lived mostly on pretty good terms with each other.

We were down near the river now. Waved to Cherokee and Abel putting some extra armor on their hogs. Crossed the bridge over the Glacier River—not wide, but a good fast stream with spring not far past—and stepped into Hanger territory.

The "Georges"—George Senior and George Junior—lived in a cabin in a tree-choked ravine half a mile downslope. For almost his whole life George's father had called him Junior, and George Junior had called himself Alphonse, a name of his own furious choosing against his father's equally furious opposition.

They argued about his calling himself Alphonse every day, with the same persistence they showed in arguing about everything else.

Mav Drood, a sweet little old spice grower just across the gorge from them, had once told me and Japh about the Georges with a vehemence that was unusual for her: "Those Georges have got more different arguments than a dog has fleas. The variety of 'em! One argument winds down, an' another one jumps right up in its place! An' they run through every single goddamn one of those arguments, every fucking day of their lives!"—this tirade uttered by Mav with a certain air of being entertained.

For decades Alphonse had lived all over the globe. He'd rather have died than come back and live with his skinny mean old fart of a father, but the hideous and insurmountable fact was that George Senior had no one else on earth who would go through the Hell of taking care of him in his old age.

At our knock he yanked open the door. The crookeder shape of George Senior stood right behind him, giving us the identical bushy-browed glare as his son. Both of them had the mad, big-pupiled eyes of hawks.

Japh spoke in his friendliest, most charming manner, eager to get everything out at once, knowing it was impossible not to anger either of these men. For starters, whichever name you called George Junior would start a row with one of them.

"Gentlemen, we're sorry to be bothering you, but we've come because you're smart and we need your help carrying some news to your friends and your neighbors." He paused, inviting an answer. Nothing. The two pairs of hawk-eyes kept glaring at him. "We'd like you to know that anyone willing to come help us fight the Studio gets—"

"Fuck yes I'm gonna fight!" gaunt, rickety George Senior bellowed. He had a powerful voice, despite his skinniness. "They're fuckin with my mountain! Some a your shit-storm's bound to splatter us! This is my place here!"

"It's my place too!" George Junior croaked (he was a heavy smoker). "I fuckin restored this place for ya! I fuckin drywalled an' painted an' porched an' decked an' re-floored an' shingled an' tiled an' re-roofed it for ya!"

"*You*? You mean you an' a buncha' other know-naught goons—an endless horde of 'em gorgin on my bread an' peanut butter an' suckin up all my beer!"

And, they were off. Japh and I hung on tight until finally George Junior paused for breath and I shouted, "Please, come up and fight with us, for acres and citizenship! Tell your neighbors. Come up tonight!"

And then we literally bolted, and left them standing there, jaws open, frozen in mid-argument.

**The sun was** half sunk, and the sky over Sunrise red now. The vehicles in the street had sprouted headlights. White sparks sprayed down from where they were welding ramps and barricades. Japh and Cap and I just stood in the street, watching it all. Jool commed me from up at Chops and Gillian's. They were making her a padded leather cuirass. I tried for a joke. "Is that to cover your ass?"

"You're the ass," she laughed. She definitely wanted me

to be snappy on this point—would stand for no "freaking out about the baby." "He's highly portable," she had lectured me. "Mammal moms fight off predators when they're this pregnant and a lot more so. Don't give me any shit about it!" I worried more for her than for the baby, which was not yet as real to me as she was. But I knew it was not in her nature to back down.

George Junior's com interrupted us. "Buncha people down here are comin up to talk to you all."

We got Smalls on it. We needed a gathering space now, and decided on the big parking area behind Cap's Hardware shared by the lumber yards and machine shops. Cap's little concrete loading dock back of his store made a natural speaking platform with good acoustics.

Just as dark fell the Hangers came up fifty or sixty strong, and the Sunrisers gave them the center of the lot. They parked their pickups and ATVS and hogs at all different angles, got out and leaned or sat on their rides, or stood in little groups in the truckbeds. Stoically listening as hundreds of Sunrisers listened all around them.

George Junior was sitting on the roof of his deformed old pickup with his legs crossed on his windshield. His own and his whole delegation's body language made it clear that he was their spokesperson.

The Hangers were a body of very opinionated and independent folks. Few of them were followers by nature, or even had much patience for views not their own. But George Junior could always just step up and spokesperson for the whole lot of them. Such was his long-ingrained paternal training in the sciences of dispute, naysaying, contradiction, and vituperation, that whenever he stood up and started proclaiming the truth about something—about anything—people just shut up and let him do it. It helped that most of his proclamations were sharp and to the point, at least when—as now—George Senior wasn't there to embroil him in argument.

His voice was a smoky caw—sounded like a big crow. He addressed himself to Smalls on the loading dock. "We can bring at least fifty to the fight. Fuck detailed arithmetic for now, but that's gonna mean about three hundred countin significant others that's gettin property up here when the fight's over, whether they wanna live full-time on it or not."

"So basically fifty or sixty households," said Smalls, talking quick to get it out before George Junior could contradict him. "You'll get fifty acres for every household, wherever they wanna choose 'em from whatever's not already taken. You join us an' fight an' you're full Sunrisers."

"What else would we be?" George squawked. "Fuckin-ay-straight full 'Risers! So first things first! Whatever kinda weapons you're gettin together, we want you to share 'em!"

"The fuck did'ja think we were gonna do?" said Smalls, and then—amazingly for this dour man—he produced a crooked little grin. "How 'bout some thirty-cal machine guns on tripods, Alphonse?"

George Junior actually blinked. "If you're not just blowin smoke up my ass," he answered, "then you're finally talkin somethin besides shit!"

The news had come to Smalls just half an hour before.

Mazy's sister Althea had a best friend named Sugi who was also close to Mazy, and had just commed her. Sugi was in Accounting at Panoply, and had just been laid off. "Listen, Maze," she said. "Mark Millar's sequel to *Somme—The Marne*—is in preproduction. They're shipping some properties to the secondary set for the shoot. Properties'll be trucked up the Five—a pretty big truck. A shipment of thirty-cals and live ammo. I mean like machine guns, belt fed!"

**We decided the** takedown of the truck could be done with four bikes and four rafts. I rode shotgun behind Christy. Just past noon, with traffic on the six lanes sparse, we came up flanking the truck on the Five down in the Valley. It was a tractor-trailer. We pulled up, two beside the truck and two beside the trailer's front wheels, hoping this would work. We didn't want to hurt the driver, but weren't sure of the physics of the situation with something this size doing ninety klicks.

We blasted the outer front wheels of the truck and the outer front wheels of the trailer. This crippled the speed of the front of the rig, and the trailer, unslowed, began to swing forward till it spanned three lanes, swinging so sharp it began to tip over.

Lance and Trek dropped their sector-boat's bows to the trailer, put some counterthrust to the teetering mass, Kate in her raft helping at the cab's tail end. It was a near thing, rubber smoking and shrieking, the big brute tilting, tilting, but then the sector-boat raft started to swing the slowing truck through a full one-eighty, till they brought it to rest in the breakdown lane aimed back the way it had come.

The driver was severely ticked, but got suddenly sociable on receiving our two hundred K. He gravely drew together his brow and said, "Yeah, I got a good look at 'em, Officer. Big Swedish-lookin bikers, Aryan tattoos. Had a rig like mine with 'em. Offloaded me with a little forklift, slick as snot!"

It was four panel trucks we offloaded him to. When the work was done I waved Kate over. "You got the time to take us for a little ride?" I asked her. She looked at me, smiling.

Since we'd fought back-to-back through the last hour of *Alien Hunger*, Kate and I were like brother and sister. She'd been a Panoply assistant director working for Margolian who had been demoted to payrafter for her reservations about Live Action just before we met. I'd tried to kill her partner when he refused to pay me for a kill, but accidently killed their raft instead. I'd helped her stay alive through the rest of that shoot, and Japh had helped too.

"A little ride? I bet I know where. Hop aboard."

Yesterday there'd been a news release from Panoply. The studio had donated nine anti-grav rafts to Sunrise ". . . to aid them in the struggle which it is Panoply's tragic duty to inflict on them."

It was a real PR coup for Panoply. And a box-office tickler: let everyone know that in this shoot there'd be an air battle to spice up the carnage. So now we could flaunt our little anti-grav fleet anywhere.

"Could it be south you wanna fly?" she asked as I strapped in. "Mr. L.A.?"

"L.A., you got that much right. But it's not that I miss the damn place. It's just that I'm used to seeing it."

"Right. I love it here, but I guess I miss its ugliness." She hit cruise altitude and set us at five hundred clicks.

"There's just one thing that interests me there. One person—my mom. Wherever she went when she left me, she's back in the Zoo, I'm sure of it."

"You miss your mom. I understand. Who wouldn't?"

"How could I miss her? I never even met her. I'm just curious."

She smiled understandingly. "Yeah. I miss my mom too."

And I had to laugh.

At five hundred it didn't take long. I'd never seen L.A. from above before. Just the beaches alone were a linear city, a snake-shaped camptown of tents and sand forty miles long. And then, the Basin! A colossal bristling blanket, wired with freeways, asphalt tentacles branching everywhere through the immensity of the Zoo.

From my 'Rise north of the Ten, I'd had wide views, but this was another order of awe. Not only the sprawl of it. From here you could really see how the Zoo's poverty had greened it, compared to photos from a couple generations back. Truck gardens, uncontrolled weed growth and tree-spread made it gorgeous as deep forest in places. A forest with a pumping, humming, internally combusting city threaded all the way through it.

Though I knew little else of my mom, I was sure she

would be in a big city. She was a seeker. But would she have come to rest in this particular city?

I couldn't help thinking so. She'd left to find some way to come back with something to offer me. All my life Auntie Drew had sworn so, and I'd always believed it. And now, if I survived, I had a life to give her.

Somehow, seeing the impossible scope of the task decided me: If I survived this shoot, I'd come back here to find her; would sure as death come back here for something else too.

"Let's scoot east for a look at the enemy," I said.

Panoply, the walled colossus, big as a city itself, lay backed up against the hills above Burbank.

"It's easy enough," I said, "for that giant to attack a little mountain town. How the hell could a mountain town attack it?"

"I think our strategy is obvious," said Kate with a little dreamy, evil smile. "The very first step would be to put out an extra-call in the Zoo. Instead of kill-bonuses, we pay them in plunder."

"Whoa!" I said, with a tingle going up my spine. "I like that!"

# XIV
## ARMAMENTS AND HAIL

**The tension on** the morning of Day Four made the air almost crackle. The 8:00 A.M. tactical meeting filled the theater and overflowed out in the street, where speakers broadcast Sandy Devlin's voice. Hundreds of natives here, men and women who'd lived with guns all their lives, listened devoutly. Whatever kind of action they'd seen, they'd never faced carnivorous man-made monsters from the maw of Hollywood.

"First, about the air battle: the sector boat packs explosive cannon, but carries a limited amount of ammo. The eight fast-rafts have machine guns fore and aft. We're going to use those primarily against APPs, but we'll do what we can against the shoot-fleet.

"It's not likely any of Panoply's shoot-rafts will be flying down within effective range of your guns, and in any case they'll have magnetic deflector-shields round their gunnels, and armored bottoms. That doesn't mean you shouldn't shoot at 'em if they happen to drop down in range. But make sure you do not fire on one of ours. Each of ours are going to have a placard on their bottom of a rising sun. We're passing it around and you people outside will get it shortly."

What soon came out was a big half-sun in Day-Glo orange.

"Armaments. Everyone fighting on foot will have two twelve-gauge pumps cut to eighteen inches, cross-holstered down their backs. Also, semi-auto forty-five caliber pistols for everyone and a belt-pack of clips. Anyone has any questions, needs any arms, your neighbors wearing these just-made Sunrise armbands can get you supplied. All you machine gunners already have your assigned emplacements—including almost every viable rooftop in town. Supervised practice ranges for all weapons are up in the Big Draw a quarter mile out Doug Fir Road.

"Now," Sandy said, "if any of you want to ask or to tell this meeting anything, let me call on you, one at a time." She looked up and saw a hand. "Jool."

Jool—already stationed down near the dais—mounted it. "I gotta say a few words."

She stood facing them all—a tight, athletic figure whose baby was beginning to show. Most of those present had seen—on screen—Jool's gift for battle in *Alien Hunger*, where much of her footage survived the final edit. And two days ago everyone present had heard her intuitions about what Val Margolian had hidden in the cinnabar mine.

"I wanna share with you all a feeling I've got. I'm not whacking out on you here, folks. I'm not starting to hear voices from the Great Beyond. But this one's really talkin to me. Panoply's got us all on dangle with this up-to-seven-days shit. It's meant to wrong-foot us by making us jumpier.

"But if you can see this, you're gonna agree that it's obvious, what day they're gonna open the ball. The first engagement—I love that word—the first engagement of Studio and Sunrise runs from sunup to midnight, right? Just picture it with me.

"The fight starts at literal sunrise, ol' Sol painting us all in gold, an' then the fight rages an' rages, with one intermission, hot an' heavy through the long day. And then there's the second intermission, as the sun starts sinking.

"The whole town's all drenched in red light and the sun's down. Then, just after the sun is set, the full moon rises above the mountains. It floods the town in moonlight.

"An' the Third Act opens, the fight comes alive again an' rages—oh so cinematically—till midnight, with the full moon at the zenith like a huge white eye looking straight down on Sunrise, and bleaching it white as a corpse."

A silence followed—in the theater, out on the street—all

those people silently seeing themselves in that grim, gorgeous horror flick Jool had just described.

Out of that silence, Devlin said, "That sounds exactly like Val Margolian to me. And that means the shoot is the day after tomorrow. So people, let's make the most of the time we've got left."

**Kate and Japh** were having a later dinner at his house by the draw. It was their first night together in two weeks. Kate was back from the acres of flowers she'd bought near the coast below Santa Cruz, where Ivy lived, her partner in the flowers. A woman most dear to Kate.

When she and Japh first became lovers, Kate was self-conscious of being the elder, being herself still young enough to think six years quite a span. She hadn't realized what a point she'd made of mating in the dark till one night Japh said, as she reached for the switch, "Wait, sweet-cake. Why don't we just put a bag over my head, put a couple holes in it so I can see, and leave the lights on? I mean I know I'm no pinup, but I haven't seen you naked for a week now."

"It hasn't been a week."

"The last four times!"

"You fool. It's not you." She lay back, brought up her knees, and hooked her elbows over them, spreading herself. "Is that naked enough?"

"Oh, Katie, you are a peach."

"Do I look bony enough for you?"

"I'm the one gettin bony here."

They'd always laughed when they made love, and in the light they laughed more—as if with recurring amazement at how wonderfully they fit together. Tonight, as her eyes got fiercer with his thrusting, he flashed on the first time he'd seen her, sliding down the steep pitch of a toppled building.

Though still a hundred feet above him, her face in its terror was indelibly clear—a long-limbed, black-haired woman with the eyes of a frightened angel. He pushed himself, pushed himself to reach her, to touch her heart, ease it, make her know she was safe, was home with him. Home.

As they lay resting, holding each other, a noise of light hail came rattling down on the house.

"Hail in midsummer?" Kate drowsily asked. "What's going on here, country boy?"—teasing as usual his birth in a 'Rise in L.A.

"Wull Mayum, ya getcher midsummer hayulls up hurr now'n then. Why I 'member one in ought six—"

Tickling, then tickle-wrestling ensued. Almost, they made love again, but for the toll of their long days' work on Sunrise's defense. Wrestling became cuddling, and sleep won them over.

But stepping out into the slant light of early morning, they saw a subtle glitter on everything. Walls, roof, deck, yard, trees—all glinted here and there. Japh opened his Buck and selected one glint from the porch column, digging it out of the redwood's soft grain.

It proved to be a minute gem. Kate, ex-assistant director, understood it at once: a lens, a micro-cam.

As his house was rigged, so the whole town proved to be, and all the homesteads around it.

With one day's preparation left, a general consensus developed: start digging them out, and there'd be no end to it. People returned to installing gun emplacements and barricades, to drilling mobile troops fighting from pickup beds or small trailers pulled by three-wheelers.

Kate got to work practicing fast crosstown manuevers with the raft squadron, skimming rooftops, dipping into the streets and out again. But she never stopped feeling the glint of those micro-cams feeding on the town's every movement.

It felt like an ant swarm nibbling her skin. She understood the "texture" this would give Val's final cut, the myriad close-ups of chaos and carnage. The whole town toiled inside one huge insect eye. . . . She thought when the shoot-fleet arrived she might fly straight up to Val and to his face call him the monster he was, scream it out for his whole crew to hear. But she knew how his eyes would mock her, mock the moral outrage of a former ex-assistant director.

Japh received a com from Cap. At the hardware store, he found Chops and Gillian already with him, helping unload heavy crates from a panel truck.

"Hefty," grunted Japh. "What's in 'em?"

"Machetes." Cap left that hanging, like a man expecting surprise.

Chops set his crate on the stack. "OK. Why machetes?"

"Close fightin. Something to pull if you lose your piece."

Chops set his crate on the stack. "Good idea for close work."

"Right."

He was talking about a moment in *Alien Hunger.*

"That's it." Cap grinned, his gold tooth flashing—and then he casually gave the finger to the street at large. It was nothing personal. People were doing the same everywhere as they worked—flipping off the micro-cams sparkling around them.

"Fangs and legs," Japh echoed. "You think it'll be another kind of bug this time?"

"Naw. Last I heard, Big Val doesn't repeat himself. Now when we get these opened, I got another little project back at the sawmill. Cause if these choppers are sorta like swords, then what about shields?"

**"The bow is** drawn, my man," Razz said to Mark. They sat over coffee in Argosy Studio's canteen, at a corner table. "And I have to tell you," he grinned, "I feel like an arrowhead, poised to slice into the flesh of the beast."

"Me too. I know what you mean. And it is a big beast, a live-action shoot. But I see what we're doing more as dropping a net on the beast."

"OK. Netting it, and then slicing its flesh."

"Razz, old friend, let's face it. You're a hot dog."

Razz grinned, "Nawww."

"Seriously. We mess with them only up to a point. Haranguing their rafts, you were right about that. Great footage there of cam-crews' faces. Their anger, their mockery, their secret shame. But we're staying out of the action, not joining it. "

"Hey. How not? I mean what do you think I've got in mind?"

"I don't know." Mark had to laugh.

"So whaddya say, is it time to join our fleet?"

**Curtis and Ricky** Dawes were laying a small-plank machine-gun platform on the roof of the Pioneer Hotel. The hotel, mostly converted to rentals for older people, was flanked by lower buildings, giving its roof a good field of fire. Below them, the streets were loud with burly three-wheelers. Some pulled trailer-beds of arms or materials or barrels of gas. Others towed little railed platforms for two shotgunners or one machine-gunner. These battle chariots were making the most noise, practicing maneuvers.

Curtis said, "Look west there, near the horizon."

". . . I don't see anything."

"Those little dots there."

Ricky saw them: a faint freckling low in the sky. And as he watched, they grew slightly bigger, and rose higher above the horizon. Word of them had begun to spread along the other rooftops.

It was a formation, wide and slender, like an oncoming blade.

They came with a calm and stately sweep, each dot enlarging to an elegant little shape, tapered and bright: polished chips of obsidian, red and black. Two hundred . . . more than two hundred anti-gravs. A grand, brilliant armada, peacefully sailing, as if come only to share with Sunrise the beauty of this mountain morning.

A roar of voices was rising from the streets. The town's fleet left off maneuvers and deployed at hover along the length of town, Trek and Lance tilting the big raft thirty degrees up from horizontal, their cannon at ready. Sandy Devlin and Sharon Harms brought their boats to hang near the roof of the hotel. Their silence, the calm of their maneuver, communicated itself to the street below them.

Sharon looked like a corn-belt farm girl and was as dangerous as a dagger. She looked down at Ricky and grinned.

"Hey, sweet thing."

Ricky, gaunt ox though he was, reddened, and had to clear his throat. "Hi Shar'n. What's happenin here?"

"Not to worry, honey bun. I believe this is just the signing."

# THE SIGNING

**Val almost wished** Mark and Razz had already deployed their pirate fleet above him now. This scene he was part of was a gorgeous opener: his formation hanging a hundred-fifty meters up, its arc as wide as the town, the day a flawless blue, the light pure gold, all the townspeople in the streets or on the rooftops, gazing skyward at his blade of rafts come to harvest their lives.

Scene One: "The Scythe Over Sunrise."

His own director's raft—grander, more blade-shaped than the rest—he dropped down to hang at thirty meters, tilting his bow down enough to display himself in his chair of power, his console of bright screens before him, his magnetic shield shimmering faintly all around the gunwales of the craft.

A two-raft delegation hung just above rooftop level below him—expecting him, apparently, to descend a bit nearer. His smile declined the invitation. Mellowly, his amped voice filled the town. "Hello, Sandy. Sharon. How delightful to see you again. It's talents like yours that have made Panoply what it is today."

He let this echo away, gazing down at them. The two pilots stared up at him, stony-eyed.

"Citizens of Sunrise, I salute you all. I'm Val Margolian. I've come to consumate the contract which we—Panoply Studios and Sunrise Incorporated—have been forced to enter into.

"I won't dishonor you with euphemisms or pretty words. Tomorrow, and the next day, in the gladiatorial spectacle we are all about to create, many of you will die. But every one of our Anti-Personnel Properties you destroy will enrich Sunrise for generations to come.

"It is Panoply Studio's melancholy honor, our sad privilege, to engage your community as both the set and the cast of its next feature, *Assault on Sunrise.* For the next two days, in the period between the sun's rise and the moon's attainment of its zenith, we will shoot three acts per day, interrupted by two substantial rest periods for Sunrise's recuperation and the repair of its defenses. I repeat that we are compelled to decry and denounce the injustice of the capital sentence we are to serve on you. But alas, in the end, the law is the law.

"Panoply expresses both its admiration for you, and its regret, with an unprecedented augmentation of payouts for each Anti-Personnel Property you destroy. Each of your kills of an APP will be recompensed with a hundred and fifty thousand dollars in cash."

He marked a pause here—an ironic hint that they might applaud this bounty if they chose. A low murmur spread through the town, sounding more like unease than anything. People wondering, perhaps, just how hard these APPs were going to be to kill. "These payments," he resumed, "will not be made in the course of the shoot—a practice which might distract and endanger you. You will receive them in full at the shoot's end.

"Ms. Devlin, I'd be honored if you were the one to signify your new allies' acceptance of this contract with Panoply Studios. Just place your hand on this palm-printer."

The little black apparatus came dangling down from his bow on a slender cable. Sandy slid her raft out to meet it, but did not yet touch it. She gazed up at Margolian a moment, and then higher, at the fleet above him. She spoke into a mike of her own, the town so still, it seemed her answer filled it and the whole sky above it.

"All of you rafters up there. I salute you as colleagues, because we have been colleagues. I have myself most surely done the work you've come to do here on us." Her bright, hard-edged voice was beautiful in the quiet mountain air. "Now it seems I'm an extra. I just can't tell you all how that changes your perspective. For one thing, I'm damn sure not gonna treat you people like colleagues. For starters I'll tell you all—straight from my heart—that if any opportunity offers, I'm going to do my level best to kill every one of you I can." She ran her eyes along the high, hovering scythe, letting her promise echo.

"Can any of you see Val's face right now, sort of fondly smiling at me? His expression seems to say, Hey. You can't make Live Action without killing, right? True enough. Just remember that goes for you too. And for you, Val. Especially for you.

"So OK. With this my own right hand, I seal our union. We, Sunrise Incorporated, take thee, Panoply Studios, in cine-matrimony."

"Cine-murder-money!" someone howled from the street, and a surf-noise of anger rose in agreement, as Sandy pressed the palm-printer and let it go. It hissed back up to Margolian's raft, and—as quick as that—Sunrise's corporate assent had been tendered to the contract.

And before Margolian's raft had risen back up to his fleet, and his fleet had turned and made its stately retreat from the sky, every adult able Sunriser was hard back at work.

**With the machetes** uncrated, and Japh gone up to work on rooftop emplacements, Chops, with a touch of unease, said to Cap, "Hey Chain."

"Hey Shackle," Cap said, and waited. Somber Chops used slam-talk only with him, whom he knew had also been Inside, and it signaled something personal.

Chops cleared his throat. "I want a badge, on the palm of my hand. You got time? It's a simple one."

Cap smiled. "I got time—got people sawing out the shields already. Step into my parlor."

The drawing Chops gave him was simple enough: the sketchy outline of an open hand, with six stars in its palm. The stars were mere asterisks, three in a horizontal line, and three at an angle below, save that the middle star in the pendant trio was a little sphere.

When he'd been working a little while, Cap said, "This rocks, design-wise. A hand in the palm of a hand."

He worked on through another silence, weighing his next words. You didn't pry on the block. Your cellie had to offer what he wanted you to know. But Gillian had shown all her friends Orion's sword.

What the hell. "You been looking through Gillian's telescope?"

Chops said, "That sphere is like a whole galaxy. It's like six billion klicks farther out, but it's lined up perfectly with two stars right here in our galaxy. And looks just the same size."

Cap smiled, very glad he'd prodded. "Maybe it's like an omen, about Sunrise. Maybe we're a lot bigger than we look to old Margolian up there."

And after some more silent work, he prodded again. "This kind of a secret? Maybe a surprise?"

Chops actually grinned. Cap had never seen him do it. "I know it'll make my hand a little sore for fightin, but the pain'll remind me."

"Of what?"

"How bad it'd hurt to lose what I got."

When Chops left, Cap went out back, and crossed to Leffert's Lumber. They'd cut out near fifty shields already, just wide-topped, taper-bottomed blanks of one-inch plywood. Fairly light, and solid. Guys with shears were making leather strips for three-ply straps. Two were to be stapled to the back of each shield—one for the forearm, one for the hand. The weight seemed just about right. Cap felt a hand on his shoulder.

"You startled the shit outta me." It was Gillian. "Hey girl."

"Can you give me an hour?" she asked him.

"What for?" But he was starting to smile, thinking maybe he already knew.

Gillian's drawing was graceful and spare of line. A wolf and a telescope. She wanted it across her shoulder.

"Tell you what," Cap told her. "I gotta settle in here real soon, but we can get it outlined, OK?"

**Late in the** afternoon Dr. Winters and Trish came up into the swarming street for a stretch. They'd been working in their basement lab for two straight days, with nearly a full day spent determining how to proceed.

They'd agreed to focus on commercial caustics and solvents because rarer substances couldn't be had in time.

But as both had feared, the gel proved impervious to any applied caustic. Liquids ran off it without any effect on its glossy surface. Getting such materials inside it involved a cumbersome procedure.

While it would aggressively seize, engulf, and dissolve any living mouse or insect that moved in its vicinity, the only way to get it to ingest inert materials was to use small bottles. The necks of these had to be sheared off at an angle with hot wires so they could be stabbed deeply enough into the gel to cause it to engulf them.

But once inside its globe, the gel simply dissolved the bottles and absorbed their contents, exhibiting no ill effects in doing so, beyond short-lived color changes in its interior. Moments later, it would expel a kind of silicaceous fluid which, when it dried on the pool-cover, became brittle like a plaque of glass.

At last—both of them sweaty, irritated, and mutely struggling with frustration, just had to get out in the air. They trudged up to the street, and out into the light of the sunset's slant rays.

The street was aswarm with activity. They stood a moment, breathing in the cool mountain air, then went round behind Cap's Hardware, and sat dangling their legs from the edge of his loading dock. Looking upslope to the east, they both knew exactly the notch in the mountains where the nearly full moon would shortly rise. Exactly where the sun too would rise, just about twelve hours from now.

Silently, they slugged it out with the gloom in their hearts. This vile, viscous invention of the studio was not going to surrender to garden-variety chemicals, and there was no way to get anything stronger in time. They absently listened to the three-wheelers roaring everywhere, the weapons reports of practice blazing away up in the hills, and heard no note of hope in the deafening noise.

As they returned to their basement, a sharp misfire from someone's old pickup jangled Winters' nerves. "Gasoline," he muttered. "We might as well try that next—it has solvent properties."

They filled a sheared-neck bottle, and stabbed a half-pint of regular into the nano-gel. The absorption of the glass occurred reliably within a few seconds of its engulfment. A brief yellowish glow ensued in the gel's interior, and faded . . . then the glassy excreta . . . nothing more.

"Shit!" screeched Trish. The young Goth had managed to belay such outbursts up till now through love of her old teacher. She strode through the crude port in the foundation wall, and into Cap's Hardware's basement for a smoke, another behavior she'd been belaying as much as she could, and for the same reason. But she got no further than taking out her lighter when frustrated rage pulled her back into the "lab." She snatched up the can, splashed the gel with gas, and lit it with her lighter—all before Winters' horror at the danger of what she was doing allowed him to make a move to stop her.

Ablaze, the gel began a violent rippling—almost a rolling boil. It bulged and puckered chaotically all over its surface and its seething mass began to shrink. Just as Winters reached for a bucket of water to douse it, the flames were snuffed out and the gel contracted to a smoking cinder, sprouting as it shrank a cluster of black spines and crooked branches.

They stood gazing at the bristly, fuming residue, less than a third its former mass and quite rigid. An indescribable chemical stench filled the air—laced, Winters fleetingly thought, with a scent of barbecue.

He told Trish, "Get Smalls. We need a tactical meeting right now—tell him just key defense people."

**Out behind the** sheriff's station, Smalls convened some two score men and women, more than half of them veteran extras. They surrounded the thorny cinder that had been the nano-gel, now lying on the pavement before them.

"Well," said Smalls out of the silence, "I damn sure don't like it and you know why. We've fielded a shitload of firearms here, and now you want gas spraying everywhere too, people strapped with tanks of it? And with all these live rounds going off?"

Ricky Dawes said, "We've just gotta take the chance. We're desperate for something we know'll hurt 'em."

"Those bug-spray tanks for gardens," offered Japh. "How many can we field?"

As the group began talking tactics and materiel, Dr. Winters' gaze kept lingering on the charred gel. He knelt close to it. "I believe," he said half to himself, "this is a tarsus. . . ."

He looked up, blinking. The whole group had fallen silent. He cleared his throat. "I believe this"—he was gingerly touching one small, crooked stalk among the black protrusions—"is a tarsus, its two terminal segments, and these are tarsal claws."

Everyone understood that the gel, in its fiery throes, had revealed some part of its programmed form, its fighting shape.

But it was Curtis, omnivorous reader that he was, who got it.

"Oh shit" he said. "It is bugs again."

# XVI
# SUNRISE BESIEGED

**In their two** director's rafts, Mark and Razz hung high, their boats gunwale to gunwale.

Razz, his handsome, Arabic profile looking devilish in the light from his instrument panel, waved at the scene below them and intoned:

*"The Assyrian came down like the wolf on the fold,*
*And their cohorts were gleaming in purple and gold;*
*And the sheen of their spears was like stars on the sea,*
*When the blue wave rolls nightly on deep Galilee."*

Mark Millar, shivering a little despite his down jacket, said, "Razz-man, you amaze me. Verse! Who is it?"

"Byron. 'The Destruction of Sennacherib.'"

"Indeed. Wow. My own take was less poetic. Let me see what I can do with it.

*Up before dawn,*
*Their faces all drawn.*
*Everyone wanting to take a nap,*
*Their butts still cold from taking their crap,*
*In outhouses on the mountainside before dawn—*
*Today they're in for a bumpy ride."*

"Not bad. You mean to say they won't be at their best today?"

"Just so, my bro."

The fleet of R and M Productions—seventy rafts—hung at three thousand feet. East of them, the first pale fan of light crowned the dark wall of the Trinities. To the west, the moon, a day off full, was half-sunk behind the western horizon. Directly below, upon the mountains' rolling foothills, spread a wide constellation of little lights: Margolian's armada, breakfasting, systems-checking, readying to take to the air and advance to their shooting position above Sunrise.

Millar murmured into his com. "Left and right wings, assume your lateral stations in ten minutes on my mark and . . . mark!"

Razz grinned, and parodied his tone: "'On my mark!' Bitchin!"

"What can I say? We're in it now, my man! Commandos! Let's go scope the enemy."

They turned east, shedding altitude as the mountains climbed under them. When they came to a hover over Sunrise, the town lay just a few hundred feet beneath their bows.

"Very very busy," Razz murmured. Sunrise was all ablaze, a great crooked candelabra of activity amid the dark trees and meadows. Headlights threaded the roads, with most going townward from the outlying homesteads, and the town's streets swarmed with movement. The partners took up binoculars.

Razz: "Whoa, machine guns on the rooftops. Where did they—"

Mark: "*Battle of the Marne*—they hijacked a shipment. Hope Val has good armor on his raft-bottoms. What have those guys on the main drag got on their backs—see there near the movie theater?"

Razz: "Some kind of packs? No—they're tanks with, like, little hoses coming off 'em. . . . Hear that?"

Mark: "A bull horn, more than one. People directing things from the rooftops maybe? Can you make out what everyone's got holstered on their backs?"

Razz: "Same thing we've got—pump-action twelve gauges, sawed-off for sure by the length. Is that a *sword* that guy's got on his hip? See him climbing the ladder to the roof of that three-story on the main drag?"

Mark: ". . . Yeah. A sword or something like it."

Upon the peaks, the sun's light was a bright crown. In

silence, the partners watched the busy protags-to-be of *Assault on Sunrise.*

Razz: "So you think the APPs are already here?"

Mark: "Don't you? It stands to reason. Two days after Val laid off all those studio people, these folks blow a mine shaft up in the hills. You can bet somebody cut loose from the Studio tipped them somethin was *in* that shaft. The APPs are in the ground where Val already had 'em planted. Now. Can he get those APPs up outta that mine again? Or has he got some other card to play?"

Razz, checking his com: "Val's going airborne! Time to go high and fall way back, let the ballet get started."

Mark: "Strike up the band!"

They shot up to five thousand, and fell back to the west again, letting a thin morning fog shield them from Panoply's flotilla, which was now rising from the plain, and gliding into its high, high hover above Sunrise. What Razz had meant by the "ballet" was the death dance with the APPs that would begin on the ground all over Sunrise, and the aerial dance of Panoply Studio's cam fleet above that embattled town, sucking up the carnage.

Margolian's armada was one vast crescent lifting from the valleys like a scythe, its leading edge slicing through a sky of tarnished silver. So stately its advance, climbing the pine-furred slopes! It took its position a thousand feet above the town, just as the sun cleared the eastern peaks: Mark and Razz dropped their rafts into the center of their own converging wings, and took the whole formation to six hundred higher still, and just behind.

"Hi, Val," Mark said softly, a nervous edge to his words, because this was the beginning of some very tricky work. They were subdivided into fourteen five-raft squadrons for independent mobility. Mark's wing was the left, Razz's the right, seven squads apiece, and each squad had its own angle to work on the shoot below. This included some close-up interactions with Panoply's rafts, so every one of their boats had a gunner aboard with a twelve-gauge. Just for show, they hoped, to forestall aggression . . .

Mark commed his wing's squad leaders—a tele-meeting, everyone's face on everyone's monitor.

He touched the detailed map of Sunrise they all shared.

"Katya," he said, "you're Sector One, this downslope piece of the north end of town." He highlighted the sector on the map. "Bound to be action on this stretch of the highway near the river bridge. Bike and automotive garages along here."

"Roger, Chief."

"Prez, you're—what is it?" Prez had turned sharply away from his monitor, looking behind him.

"Sorry Mark." The man faced him again, presenting a sheepish smile. "I thought I heard—" with a yelp he wrenched himself violently offscreen. Mark turned for a visual down along his wing. At its tip, too far for details, he saw a half-dozen rafts breaking rank, some upward, some down.

"Maiko! Pick up! What's Prez—"

Maiko's face thrust into the vacated screen. "Mark! We've got bogies! Prez is dead!"

But Mark was now seeing it all along both wings, as Razz was on his own monitor. Their rafts were breaking formation above and below, while everywhere—what the fuck *were* those things? Big and shining, long skeletal legs dangling under them, black, streamlined bodies flexing and twisting . . . harrying his boats. He hit Code Red Alert and commed every craft, "Go high, go high, hit two K!"

All went vertical, but were scarcely five hundred feet higher when it was clear that their fleet was alone in the air, and their assailants nowhere in sight.

Razz's and Mark's eyes met on-screen, and with one grim look they agreed that this moment must be seized and twisted to their will, or they would lose everything here and now.

Razz commed, "All craft listen up. Whatever just hit us is the same thing's going to be hitting Sunrise down there just minutes from now. Here on out, those things won't have time for us. I know you're scared, but listen hard. We are *holding* six hundred mil right now on a right of first refusal to this groundbreaking, this *millennial* vid-of-a-shoot we're about to shoot. Record what I'm gonna say—it's a *contract.*

"Every one of you sees this through, at shoot's end gets a million cash in pocket within twelve hours' time, and a sixteenth point of the gross. You heard me right. Mark and I want fame, and we're willing to pay for it."

He took a deep breath; everything rode on the crew's reply. "Hit your squawk button now if you want down and out."

Razz waited through a silent slow count of five. "All right. Silence is consent. Balls or whatever, you've all *got* a pair."

"Ovaries, asshole," a woman said on the open line, and some laughter ran through the formation.

A further moment's silence followed, as people met their crewmates' eyes, sealing their consent.

"OK then," said Mark. "Cover and belay your dead. They'll take the rest of this wild ride with us, and their families get their shares. Let's buckle down and steal this son-of-a-bitch's vid from him."

By the time the sun's first blaze edged over the peaks, Mark and Razz had determined that their dead numbered thirty-one, and that no boat had less than two crew. They were good to go.

**They'd wanted to** shoot his shoot, but he had shot theirs first. Smiling a wintry little smile, Val Margolian checked his APP feeds. It was the twenty he'd wakened early that he scanned, his welcoming committee for Mark Millar's little flying circus of vid-thieves. They'd caught some damn good footage. How swift they were, how slow their human prey crumpling under their lightning strokes. At present, those APPs' visual input registered nothing but shadows and pine boughs, for he'd hidden them, hugging the trunks of the trees below town.

It would be a nice shot of them, swarming up from behind just when most of the town would be turning to face the main host flying down from the hillsides. That would be a nice touch. If Mark, that greedy skulker, hadn't come thieving, Val would never have thought of such a redeployment. Improvisation was the spice of art.

The sun's rim seared the sky above the peaks, its slant shafts striping the town in gold and shadow. This was technically sunrise, but that orb, like the moon's, took eleven minutes to rise one full diameter.

*Let's wait a bit.*

How much better this was than people galloping pell-mell into a studio set! See them there pausing in the midst of desperate preparation. Look how they waited, frozen, weapons in hand, others bent over their not-quite-completed defenses. Everyone united in sudden suspense, in cruel last-minute doubt of all their contrivances and calculations. Here was Everyman, facing not unreal monsters, but Fate itself.

Now? No, a few minutes more.

He hung there savoring this imminence—not of a carnivorous mêlée, but of battle. He'd been lucky to get his raft-bottoms armored in time once he'd learned of the town's machine guns, but had done it in time too short for lightweight work, for dura-lacquer laminations. He'd made do with metal, and his boats were bottom heavy, slightly but distinctly slower in tight maneuvers than Devlin's tiny raft squad. Devlin. That sly little bitch. She'd get some special APP attention, but meanwhile he'd have to—

Movement in the eastern sky. From a thousand feet up, straight out of the sun's growing glare, an arrow of rafts dropped down on his boats from eleven o'clock high, machine-gun fire blistering the morning quiet. It was near-vertical fire and his rafts' deflector-shields walled but did not roof them. The thirty-cal poured into the cockpits of raft after raft.

Val's pilots snapped to, tilting their craft bottoms-out as they peeled from Devlin's squadron's dive-path, but two—with only dead meat at their helms—plunged on rudderless, one skyward, but the other—angled down—crashed into the legs of the water tower and lodged there. Two of Devlin's rafts whipped back to it, and they already had a pilot aboard it while Margolian's fleet-monitors were registering casualties. A dozen . . . no, fifteen people lay bleeding aboard his boats, some surely dead. All this while he keyed his army awake, his fingers flying to pluck them up into the sky.

His APP displays, all dark, began to show glints of light and dim hints of mass in motion. Soil and turf hatched outward, and admitted still more light. Sky appeared, fringed with grass blades. And then, as his terrible children shouldered free of the earth, the whole green mountainside, the golden sky, the great gilded trees gently stirring in the morning breeze—all this flooded into their jeweled eyes, and thence onto his display.

Each hatchling saw its brethren hatching all about it now, all those globed eyes encompassed by a hall of mirrors, all echoed by themselves a hundredfold on every side. Each of Val's screens was a sprouting jungle of jeweled heads and now—like flashing swords unsheathed from the turf—arose their great wings whose whirr slashed rainbows from the sunlight and lifted . . . lifted from the soil gaunt sleek bodies, spare machinelike legs and—lastly—tapered stingers curved like sabers, black as death.

The hum of their ascension filled the air, growing louder each second. *Beautiful.* Val grimly smiled, and commed the fleet.

"Action," he said.

# ACTION

**Margolian's armada swept** out of the west. On the roof of the Masonic Temple, Japh prayed that all their improvisations would work. Two hundred pairs of foot patrol on the sidewalks, one of each pair with a gas sprayer, and flanking the sprayer, his gunner. A blast of hot buckshot had seemed like the quickest way to ignite a gas-sprayed body, but would it work?

The whole mid-street was cleared for their armored vehicles: gnarly pickups with gunners in the beds, midsize flatbeds for resupply and rescue of wounded. Wheel Right choppers threaded among them, their sidecars carrying more gunners. All windshields had been covered with patches of chain link, ditto all headlights for the two night battles. The guys in the truckbeds carried equal arrays of twelve-gauges and forty-five cal Thompson submachine guns. Heavy arms, but would they work on what they'd be facing?

Meanwhile every flat rooftop, and even some peaked ones where ladders and platforms were rigged, had a machine-gun nest like Japh's own. Not an angle of any street they couldn't sweep from on high, or surveil to shout warnings to fighters below.

So many people so dear to him here, and all this firepower. He scanned the invaders' raft-bottoms paving the sky. Armored for sure, magnetic deflectors fencing their rims. There was no hurting *them* with bullets, but what about themselves? All these weapons locked and loaded, muzzles blazing, tracking targets moving fast . . .

What control did you really have in the heat of a fight? Even now the rooftop gunners were calling back and forth, defining "fire zones" to which each gun would confine its rounds. Yeah, right, once the fight was at full blaze.

"Hey, Soldier!" Kate Harlow slid right up beside him on her raft. "Cover your eyes," she said to her tail gunner. She leaned out and wrapped her arms around him.

He held her in his right arm, stroking her head with his left hand. This was his "new" hand. Its tactile wiring was state-of-the-art, but still not quite *true*. To his prosthetic fingertips, the texture of her hair, the softness of her nape were a shade less distinct, felt sketchier, as if she was, or was becoming, a ghost.

He hugged her harder, making her laugh and say, "Don't crack me, big guy."

"You be careful, Kate."

"It's Val's gotta be careful, lover. We've got a treat for him."

They kissed. Such a complete promise a kiss was. But when their lips parted, there was only its fading warmth. The ghost of a kiss. Kate skimmed away, hooked into an alley, and left his view.

Japh stood there, afraid for her, afraid for every soul in Sunrise. He remembered those seconds on the set of *Alien Hunger* just after the spider had injected its venom into his forearm. How many ghosts were left there, on that set, by the time those monsters had done their work?

There was one thing you could count on Margolian for: nightmares. Thank god Curtis had been there. Only he would have had the nerve to swing his axe without an instant's pause, and chop Japh's sudden death right off his arm.

Japh came back to the present and like everyone else stood watching the sky. Above Margolian's armada, a second formation had appeared, much smaller, hanging hundreds of feet higher. Auxiliary forces? Why so much higher? The light in the east said sunup was imminent. What was Margolian up to?

Then a hundred voices shouted, "Look!" A thousand feet up, swift bright blurs—too fast and too vague to identify—were rising toward that higher fleet and . . . were striking them. Tumult rocked their formation, its members dancing crazily in and out of pattern.

Whatever the blow they had received, it was delivered in moments, and the rafts jostled back into pattern. A thousand Sunriser brains struggled to unwrap this enigma. Margolian's scythe had taken no similar blow . . . so maybe it had delivered it? Were the higher boats interlopers? Were they cam-rafts like Panoply's?

Were they stealing his vid as he shot it?

"They came to shoot the shoot!" Japh shouted. "Vid-thieves! And . . . Margolian's used his APPs on them! They're airborne! These APPs can *fly*!"

There was a flurry of activity among the rooftop gunners as they readjusted their machine guns' tripods and platforms. The armored vehicles began to mount guns up on the roofs of their cabs. . . .

And as everyone worked, a realization spread through the town. Where was their own little airforce? None of the town's airboats were anywhere in sight.

They were still gone as the clock ticked down, and people manned their readjusted weapons, and stood poised again. . . .

The first blaze of the sun flared from the peaks of the Trinities. But the solar torch kindled . . . nothing. Not a stir from Panoply's fleet. Not one monster, airborne or earth-born—just perfect poise and silence. Just that motionless host growing golden in the light of morning.

And the besieged, without one lifted voice, shared in

perfect silence the same understanding: that this stillness above them was a sneer, was Margolian sardonically tipping his hat to them.

Every soul in Sunrise felt through those long moments a greater rage than any war cry could have roused. Then their own small air force made an answer for them. Out of the blinding arc of the rising sun, their boats plunged like bolts from a crossbow, machine-gunning Panoply's rafts from overhead.

"Back 'em up!" howled Japh.

Every machine gun opened up, powerless to harm the fleet, but hammering it with impacts and distracting its pilots while the Sunrise Airborne strafed the fleet from topside. Lance and Trek's sector boat with its cannon visibly jolted each boat it hit and knocked two craft right out of formation, making one crash in the water tower's legs.

Silence then. Japh watched the home team streak back to defensive formation just above town. They'd bitch-slapped Margolian and now the shit would hit the fan.

He looked up the slopes. Those meadows, those noble congregations of grandfather pines glinting with the sun's gold on their crests. How he loved this place, the taste of the air, the scent of the endless green life. It was lucky he hadn't yet gotten his parents up here, but if he was still standing when this was over he by-god would.

He sent up a prayer for all those he loved up here. He could feel how it had heartened them all that Sunrise had drawn first blood. A murmur of energy hummed through them and readiness seethed in the streets. Sunrise had spilt first blood, and took heart from it. The dragon had bled and its blow would come any time now. . . .

"From the east!" someone screamed. "From the hills!" Japh swung his gun round and began to fire into the host that came whirring down.

Like black angels they dove, each in its own golden blur of shining wings. Lean, jointed bodies they had, dangling long, skeletal legs and, amidst these, a slender stinger curved down.

Something dreadful in those bodies' stillness as they hung so poised upon their wings' dire energy.

Japh's tracers streaked out to meet them, all his fellows' fire raging round him. He felt big-caliber death hum past his skull—an ally's misdirected shot. He slung himself down on his belly, and continued firing prone.

**When it seemed** that the gunfire had been thundering forever, Jool saw her first APP outside one of the stained-glass windows of the Church of the Blessed Redeemer.

She and Gillian were two of the five women patrolling the church's aisles with submachine guns held at port-arms—port-arms in Jool's case meaning lightly resting atop her slight belly, whose girth was increased by the thick flak-vest she'd donned to protect it. Momma Grace and Auntie Drew flanked the church doors with twelve-gauges.

The other forty-seven women and children were deployed amid the pews. All these—and there were others like them in other refuges—were diehard home-fronters who'd refused evacuation, many with firearms propped on the pew-backs.

She and Gillian took comfort in their fellow Thompson-wielding women. Kathy and Meegan were Rasmussens, nieces of Elmer. Back when they were settling in, before the firestorm started, lean, squint-eyed Kathy had announced to the room:

"Hey you guys. You know me an' my sis here. I just wanna say we're sorry for clocking those corp cops. I know I personally put paid to one a them sonsabitches, though it took me more shots with a bolt-action than it woulda done with one a these sweet pieces we got now."

"*You* killed him?" squawked Meegan from the next aisle over. "Was *me* took the top of his head off 'fore your slug ever touched him!"

"Girls! Ladies!" This was the fifth Thompson lady, Miss Louella Wells, gray-haired and rifle-straight. She'd still been Principal of Sunrise High when the Mlles. Rasmussen had, occasionally, attended it. Since retirement she'd studiously pursued her two passions: raising flowers and hunting deer. "We're all sure you *both* killed him, and we're all sure you had no choice. They were a snare set for us all. Now we have some much more serious killing to do."

After the words "set for us all," Jool saw, or thought she saw, a number of eyes flick toward her. She blurted, "Listen. All of you. I was an extra. At Panoply. A lot of us feel that our presence—"

"You stopped being an extra," Miss Wells overrode her cooly, "when you came here. Now you're a Sunriser, and that means—" She paused. The first rays of sunlight had just struck the stained-glass windows. "And that means," Miss Wells resumed, "our lives for yours, dear. That's all there is to it."

Tears jumped to Jool's eyes. "And our lives for yours," she said. "Our lives for yours." And thought, the moment after, of her small companion under the flak jacket.

Long minutes passed, and then, machine-gun fire from somewhere in the sky. A long moment followed, and a longer one. Then all hell broke loose outside from what sounded like every rooftop in town.

The APPs had arrived. She wanted to com Curtis on the roof over their heads, but dared not distract him. Her ears, though ringing, still sifted the pandemonium outside for clues to what was happening, and it seemed to her that almost all the fire came from the rooftops, and most of the firepower down in the street had yet to come alive.

And then it did. Shotguns and automatics awoke right beyond the church doors, echoing between the shopfronts while their spent casings clattered on the pavements everywhere.

A big shadow dropped into view just outside the church's big stained-glass window. There, where the Virgin Mother's head inclined tenderly downward, gazing on the Infant on her lap, the hovering shape outside dimmed the color from the Madonna's face and shoulders. It rose and sank gently in its airborne position, a long, horizontal silhouette, bi-partite, the forepart bulkier than the tapered rear while—eerily audible within the stuttering roar of gunfire—a purring buzz seemed to come from it.

Until, in the same instant, the shadow rose sharply and the top of the window exploded beneath it in a rainbow spray of shards.

In the void left by the Virgin Mother's destroyed head and shoulders, they saw plainly an alien shape of black and silver in the sun: a huge wasp hanging on the air, a dire, gorgeous thing: death perfectly designed.

Jool's and the other four Thompsons opened up in almost the same instant, hammering it fore and aft, spraying its black tissue into the sunlight, while the gun outside that had just missed it, aimed from more directly underneath, now sent gouts of its substance geysering skyward.

Yet still it flew, slid sideways, upward, and—horribly distinct in the golden sunlight—reknit, the ragged holes torn in its thorax and abdomen shrinking, closing, the entire creature contracting slightly in its self-repair.

As it slid high and out of view, the sunlight flashed off the long, glossy spike of its sting. And through the portal the wasp had vacated, the women saw a piece of sky that swarmed with its brethren.

Jool heard amid the mêlée the fragment of a hoarse shout above them. Curtis's voice, from up on the church roof. "Rake!" she thought she heard him howl. ". . . Behind you!"

# XVIII
# THE FIRST MOVEMENT

**Giant bugs—we** knew that already. But airborne!

And how hard was that to forsee? Damn few bugs don't have wings. The fucking spiders had been bad enough, but at least they had to run you down to kill you.

These bugs streaked down and froze midair, shifting a little side to side—almost like good old Margolian just wanted to give us a look at them before they killed us. I laid thirty-cal on them. Chunks whicked off their legs, wings, bodies. They zig-zagged clear, reknitting on the wing, their torn parts—slightly smaller—sprouting back. I looked at these things and I saw in them Margolian himself—his ugly will, his twisted mission. Always the entertainer, he didn't just like killing us, he liked wowing us too.

Their heads were huge eyes, two faceted hemispheres flashing rainbow in the sun. Margolian was feasting on us with these eyes, all cameras, of course, that sucked us up, spread us out up there on his monitors, where he could watch us crouching and ducking and desperately gunning. The thoraxes were bulky and angular and looked muscle-bound dangling their long segmented legs. The abdomens were fat and sleek, arcing out and down to their saber-like stingers.

But showtime was over. Now they were coming at us everywhere, our gunfire zipping up through them like a vertical blizzard. We were trimming a hail of frags off them that melted midair back to gel and spattered down on our roofs and pavements.

Their stingers were lightning-quick and people were down everywhere. We couldn't find a rhythm for defense. Bobbing and hovering, zigging and zagging they filled the air, but when they dove to sting they were sudden and quick as thrown knives.

I was up here to protect the church but I couldn't cover the front of it—the street forces had to do that. I worked to nail everything that even came near it, but now and then a bug dropped past me. Then, was that a window shattering beneath me? And after that, gunfire pouring *out* of that window?

I couldn't go down to her, couldn't leave their airspace

uncovered—could only send prayers with each round that they fired.

"Rake!" I screamed to a friend on a rooftop across the street. "Behind you!"

It nailed him in the upper back. He went slack, his astonished eyes fixed on mine, still standing because the wasp, like a skyhook, held him upright. I laid fire on it, but it hung there shedding chunks while its abdomen pulsed, and pulsed again. It dropped him then and climbed, healing as it rose.

They nailed one at last down on Glacier—drenched it with gas as its stinger was sunk in a victim, and gunned it alight. It went high all afire.

You could only call clenching what the fucker did then. Its body contracted, turned black and crusty and absorbed the flames. A smoking cinder with wings still whirring it hovered, and then raining off it came a shower of ash and the bug rose intact again, smaller perhaps by a third. Torching didn't work on them!

Bullhorns were blaring, "Blobs! Watch your feet!" I saw 'Manda Drake, a woman that Momma'd been tutoring, writhing on the ground with gel globed round her foot. The guy that snatched her up slipped on another blob, almost falling as he dragged her clear. And because we couldn't stop firing, gel just kept raining down on us.

And every so often I couldn't help looking up at the Studio's cam fleet sucking up every tick of this carnage. You could see them working, their whole formation seething as each boat shifted or tilted or rose or dropped for its camera angle, a huge flock of carrion birds feasting midair on our photons.

All was delirium. I was hammering monsters to pieces that flew back together, and the roar of my gun erased my mind. And as my brain went away my gunning got truer, my tracers a half-beat ahead of their movement and I was nailing them, nailing them just as they got there. I had one now, was tearing away at its upper thorax, and I kept it pinned just long enough that its head flew off.

Head and body dropped like stone—a fifty-foot fall, and both parts had reverted to gel before impact.

"Take off their heads!" I screamed to the town. Screamed it again. Did anyone hear?

I tried to do it again, but now that I was trying I couldn't seem to manage it. We were all in unison once more, a town-size storm of gunfire that brought down nothing but a rain of gel spattering the streets. And that gel kept rivering, meeting, and merging. There were globs of it prowling everywhere underfoot.

And then there were no wasps in the streets anymore. They all hung at hover well above roof level. They dove and feinted and pulled back up. Drawing our gunfire aloft but no longer engaging.

It was like a musical pause. Panoply was setting a tempo, playing our town like an organ. Now it was filming our recovery work, the damage control we all had to turn to the instant this moment allowed it. Bullhorns called for fire control. Gas had sprayed wild from pump-gunners trying to drench diving targets, and hot shot had set the porch of the library on fire along with some walls here and there.

Other horns blared for medevac. This was grim work. There were casualties like Amanda—a guy who'd reached behind himself to break his fall and now had gel up to his elbow, and a few others losing feet or legs even as we carried them off for amputation. But apart from these, "medevac" meant carrying stone-dead Sunrisers back to the industrial zone, and laying them out in the big lot beside the lumber mill. One hit from those stingers and you were stone dead.

"Hey Curtis!" Cap, down in the street, had to shout because we had gunners still working the sky. There was a gash on his head and he was bleeding from both arms, his own blood on the grip of his machete. His shield looked hammered and splintery on the front.

"How're those workin, Cap?"

"They work! Lock up their stingers, but we can't kill 'em. Their legs tear ya up while you're tryin to chop 'em. Cut off their stingers an they fly up an grow another. Half my guys quit, went back to guns. I heard you killed one!"

"Yeah! Shot its *head* off! Pass that around!"

He had to dodge as he ran off, because the wasps were coming down again. We'd already lost dozens of friends. Our score so far: one. My lucky shot.

**Act Two was** over. The sun was near the far western hills. A chill breeze dried our sweat and made us shiver.

Japh and I were carrying a corpse out into the industrial zone—a big older guy, a Hanger whose name we didn't know. We were tired to the bone, and black-grim at heart, and both of us trying not to let the other see it. The dead seemed so heavy, and we were so tired.

"Little closer, Curtis," Japh said. We laid him up tight against the outermost body, one more flagstone in a pavement of dead. There was need of close stacking. The first rank lay tight to the side of the mill, and four more ranks lay beside that. More than a hundred dead, and at least fifteen people unaccounted for.

The battle had flowed out here in the Second Act. To have foot room for fighting we'd have to start laying the next act's casualties two-deep.

Along Glacier Avenue, tired fighters huddled on porches and slumped back against walls. People circulated on bicycles carrying wine and water and bread and cheese for those not too exhausted to eat.

We walked in a kind of trance. When the APPs had swarmed off to the hills, amped voices from the shoot-rafts had called Intermission until full moonrise, more than two hours off. It seemed like a new kind of time we were walking through, where you could look around and draw an easy breath.

Japh went to find Kate and I started for the church to see Jool and our ladies. Everyone was OK. No APPs had gotten in, but a lot of gel was blown off them that'd made things risky underfoot in the church. We'd dragged the dormant stuff out before we'd sat down to rest together.

I commed her now as I headed back over there.

"Just come here, hon. Just come here," she told me, and

clicked off. I heard bad news in her voice. I started jogging. I saw from a couple blocks off that everyone had come out of the church and were grouped on the sidewalk.

She stepped out of the crowd to meet me, wrapped her arms around me and held on like a limpet. I knew now it was either my auntie or her momma, and then I saw Momma Grace weeping there, being comforted by Gillian, and Jool was saying to me, "I'm so sorry, hon. I'm so sorry."

I don't remember going inside the church—only standing beside the pew they'd laid her on. Her tight little face in its white puffball of hair looked like she'd gone to sleep angry and the anger was just fading out of her features as her sleep got deeper.

Her left leg was gone to the knee. She looked so small . . . and I realized that my auntie *was* small and always had been. And that it was only her fierce little mind, and the love in her, that had made me see her as larger all my life, even when I was nearly twice her size.

I knelt down and took her in my arms and let the tears come. Tears don't help at all—that's why they're tears. But somehow when they've fallen they do help. They help to collect in your heart all you've lost.

I remembered her so pissed at me she smacked my hand with her mixing spoon for scooping out the dough with my fingers, and I remembered laughing at her for even *hitting* me gently. It made her laugh too, ticked though she was.

I remembered so clearly the morning she taught me what *reading* was. The sun was pouring through the window, and here on my lap was my pal, *The Poky Little Puppy.*

And here was Auntie's finger, touching these little marks below my pal, and saying a word with each one she touched. And it hit me: these little marks were talking to me, *me*, about the Poky Little Puppy!

I remembered the first bad fight I'd gotten into at school in the fifth grade. We'd both gotten pretty colorful, and the principal had really reamed us out about it, and Auntie had already been called when I got back home. There was thunder and outrage in her eyes, and she wouldn't say a word to me, just started cleaning up my cuts and scrapes and none too gently either. I felt pretty low.

Then she went and stood by the window, glowering. I realized years later that she was thinking of when she'd been eleven, down there in the Zoo. She'd worked long and hard to get from down there up to here, but she was trying to recapture that long-ago girl down there and trying to find what to tell me.

She came and sat down in front of me and took my right arm and squeezed my wrist.

"Yow!"

"I know it hurts, Curtis. See how swollen it is? That's because you didn't keep your wrist straight. Give me your left hand. Now hold that wrist straight with your elbow like this. Now throw that whole arm with your punch with your back in it too."

Of all the things she gave me, maybe that was the hardest for her.

Jool knelt near me. "Listen. People who've . . . lost parts

to the gel. They say it's not pain, just cold and pressure. We think it's just shock that . . ."

"That killed her." I nodded, trying to let her know it helped that there had been no agony in her passing. I laid Auntie back down on the pew and touched her face with both my hands, and drew them back. This touch, this sensation on my palms, was the last I would ever have of her. I said good-bye to her. I knew I'd be saying it for the rest of my life.

Japh was there. When he hugged me, I found I had more tears for her in me. So did Japh. He'd stolen her cookie-dough too. . . . We wrapped Auntie in blankets, carried her back to the altar, and laid her near it.

**As they walked** together over to the theater, Japh asked Curtis, "Whaddya make of those?" Here and there along the street lay actual dead APPs—beheaded wasps that had not gone to gel, but lay like little wrecked planes on the pavement.

Curtis didn't answer. Japh gripped his shoulder and answered himself. "I think it's just cinema myself. For the visual effect. A lull in the battle, tired Sunrisers clearing the wreckage, and in the streets, dead monsters here and there. Their cams never sleep, right?"

"Margolian. I'm gonna tear that sonofabitch's throat out."

"We both are."

More than half the crowd in the theater were asleep, in

chairs or curled on the floor. Others leaned or lay resting, in a buzz of low, tired talk with their neighbors . . . or holding them as they wept.

"Anyone sleeping, let 'em," Smalls said. "Then we'll all do some sleeping in shifts. First the good news. Best we can figure, we've killed at least eighty of those sonsabitches—no offense ladies—an' maybe more. Thank god for Cap's swords-an-shields. We had fifty workin it by last act's end, but he's got the gear for a lot more teams and we're gonna field 'em next act. Gunners keep working the air and those that come divin at you, but when they get in close enough we're gonna decapitate 'em.

"Remember, when those APPs nail that wood, lean into them to snag 'em and tilt that shield hard, twist that stinger to lodge it in the shield. And you machete folk get in there quick and swinging hard. Cap, we got a lot to thank you for."

"We're makin more in the mill right now," Cap said. "Listen—hear that?" And they could—a faint shriek from two blocks away: Cap's machetes bleeding streams of sparks from the grinding wheels.

Ricky Dawes had just come in, looking glum. He raised a voice gravelly with fatigue. "I think it's the ones've already stung someone we're mostly draggin down. We had two break away from us, but the others we got just after they'd nailed someone. Like the stinging had weakened 'em maybe."

"Fuckin high price to pay for a kill," someone growled.

"Yeah," sighed Ricky. He threw a hesitant look at the people around him. "Can I get up there a minute?"

When he had, he cleared his throat and looked at us all. From under his shaggy brows, his eyes seemed a tired old coyote's, a friendly enough dog, but one who had some bad news for his pack-mates.

"Well first, I don't want you all to think I'm—what's that word for someone that thinks he's gonna be, like, defeated?"

"Defeatist," several voices offered.

"Right. I don't want you to think I'm a defetus, but I think we have to by-god decide right now that whoever of us gets through this fight tonight, has to get busy, get ATVs together, and get every woman and girl out of this town a hundred miles gone before sunrise—no! No! No offense! I just mean . . ." Ricky was shouting his last few lines because of all the women shouting at him: "Fuck You! You run! C'mere an' I'll whip your ass for you!"

"Just please listen!" he shouted. "And I mean all the young men too, I mean all the ones under eighteen should go, because we want Sunrise to survive, and I don't think anyone stays in this shoot is gonna. I mean, survive. I'm really sorry, but our dead count's lookin way off. We been like, tallying, an' there's like twelve, maybe fifteen people we can't account for, that it's lookin like gel musta got 'em. I mean just the loose gel they melt down to when you chop 'em up! And we got as many more too crippled to fight. And tonight in the dark's gonna be the worst fight yet, an that'll just be half the battle. And . . . we'll fight the second day on five hours' sleep."

Ricky's voice got quieter toward the end, because the whole big room had done the same.

Smalls said, "Thanks Ricky. We all had to look at it. When it's time, we'll look at it again. Please all do some sleeping if you can."

# XIX
## A BARBECUE

**Curtis trudged back** toward the church, to check on Jool. The street was half cleared of bodies and debris . . . but here came a congested stretch where the patrol vehicles had to go to one lane around a big flatbed. The truck had a tension scale on the tail of its bed. Near were gathered a number of the headless APPs that had not gone to gel, and Dr. Winters seemed to be weighing them.

Curtis paused to watch him as he directed two men to hoist an APP between them. He set the scale's load hook around the crooked tubular segment joining the wasp's thorax and abdomen. The springs creaked and Winters said something to Trish, which she keyed into her com.

"Hey Doc," said Curtis. "You got any idea why these ones didn't melt?"

"Not likely to be a glitch in the programming. Must be some purpose to it."

"We think the Studio wanted the visuals—the alien dead lying with our dead, monsters' bodies mingled with our own, et cetera."

"Whatever the reason, Curtis, we're finding them very . . . informative. Is there a sizeable crowd in the theater?"

"Yes. Mostly sleeping."

"They'll have to wake up. We all need to discuss something. We'll be there in a minute."

Curtis went on to the church. Found Jool and Gillian awake and flanking Momma Grace with their arms around her shoulders. Momma Grace had fallen asleep between them, the tears on her face not quite dried, and the young women spoke gently to one another across her sleeping form, sensing that their voices comforted her grieving dreams. Women and youngsters were asleep all around them. He slipped in beside her. "You should both clock some z's"—keeping his voice low—"there's an hour and a half still left for it."

"Lemme talk to my girlfriend, Curtis," Jool murmured. "She saved my life."

Gillian smiled, "We've been savin each other's life all day long."

"Hush, I've been knowin you a while girl, but I'm feelin you now."

Curtis kissed Jool, and touched Gillian's shoulder. "Then I'm feelin you too, Indian girl. I'm just gonna close my eyes a minute, gotta get back to the Majestic. The Doc has something to tell everyone. . . ."

And a moment later, Jool smiled sadly, feeling his head sag to her shoulder. Asleep. She stroked his cheek and whispered, "Sleep hon. Heal your heart."

**Dr. Winters and** Trish came into the Majestic muttering to each other, and mounted the dais still talking in an undertone. Gentle wake-ups were murmured through the room, and not a few awakened with a groan, or a yelp. Oddly—perhaps merely forgetfully—Trish had a gas tank and hose hung on her shoulder. Dr. Winters greeted his audience with the easy address of a thirty-year teacher.

"Friends, we've been weighing the wasps, and trying to answer a question their bodies have raised for us. Let's start with the fact that their weight's not uniform. They're all identical—they don't vary in size, or in any structural way at all, but the weights of our specimens vary within a range of thirty-five kilos. This is a fairly remarkable range because it makes individuals at the low end thirty percent lighter than those at the upper end."

"It's the poison's weight," said Laoni Meeks, one of the lean, solemn women who ran sheep on the lower slopes. "They pump it in three, four seconds at a hit."

"The same thought occurred to us, Laoni. But let's save that, because I want to consider just their overall mass for a moment. We've examined a random sampling of ten individuals. This group contained four top-weight individuals. Of the other six, two weighed about twenty kilos less, and the rest, nearly forty—some thirty percent of their maximum mass. This is scant data, of course, but Trish and I are convinced of its meaning. We think the differences relate to the number of times our samples struck prey. The heaviest, we think, were beheaded before they struck anyone. When they do strike, we believe the wasps are injecting significant quanta of their mass into their victims."

He paused with a solemn air, as if expecting a general reaction. Complete silence greeted his revelation.

"My friends," Winters said, showing just a touch of exasperation, "surely you've noted that these are ichneumonid wasps. They are modeled—except for their large heads and eyes—on Megarhyssa." And, after another silence, "Oh, why did so few of you come to my Biology One!? Never mind. Never mind. Ichneumonids oviposit their prey. Their young devour the hosts from inside."

"Their young . . ." said Smalls in the silence, his voice rusty from his absorption in these words.

"We can only speculate," Winters said, sounding gentler now, "but it stands to reason. We've destroyed probably eighty wasps. Body parts they lose while alive, so to speak, revert to base-mode gel, and enough of this is loose in town to pose a serious threat. A score of people have lost hands or feet, and we're pretty sure more than a dozen have been entirely ingested. Some sizeable masses of gel have coalesced and will be actively hunting. Still, raw gel just won't provide the large-scale homicide they want for their cameras.

"Can the studio sustain losses like this, and still have a movie tomorrow? I'm sorry to say, I don't think they're worried about that. I'm very much afraid that our fallen friends may be the . . . source of new enemies tomorrow, and when tonight's fight is over, we'll have to surround their bodies with guns and gas."

He had to raise his voice at the end, because everybody was talking now, their voices quickly rising to a roar.

"I'm sorry!" the doctor shouted, and had to shout it again and again. And when at last he had silence—except for the sound of people sobbing here and there, he said once more, "I'm sorry. Our dead were dear to us, are dear to us. What's been done to us was not done by men, but by monsters, human monsters worse than these they've sent against us. But as I believe that a second wave of killers is growing in those dear ones we've lost, we must be ready to incinerate them the moment they emerge."

"The gas doesn't work," someone cried. "It shrinks 'em and they shed the ash!"

Surprising many in that room, Trish piped up. "Not necessarily! We wanna try something." She blinked, as if startled by her own boldness, little professional skulker and outsider that she was. "We want four or five people to help us out."

Cap and Chops stood up. "Atcher service," said Cap. Winters was going to speak, but Trish spoke first—finding her stage presence, it seemed. "We've got over an hour. We wanna try . . . like an experiment. Everyone that can should just keep resting up."

Ricky Dawes and Laoni joined them, and the six trooped outside.

**They crossed Glacier,** all looking behind them at one moment or other up to the eastern peaks. Was that a faint hint of silver light dawning? Trish led them to the concrete steps down to West Glacier, a narrower, residential street downslope. Over her shoulder she said, "We had people tracking it near the end of the battle because it was so big. They said just before shutdown it went into that house there, where the door was standing open."

It was a high-porched, modestly ornamented little two-story. As they climbed the steps, a touching domestic smell wafted out of it, of lavender and dried rosemary. They paused at the door, pulling it all the way open, beaming their lights inside. The little atrium and half the parlor it flanked showed stark, webbed with shadows. On the parlor's flowered rug sat a grayish, oblate spheroid, murkily luminous within. Its bulk squatted almost waist-high to Trish, who hesitated a few steps from it. "They didn't say it was this big . . . Ohmy-god! There's something behind it!"

It was the hindquarters of a dog—a big shepherd, by the legs and tail. The stump of its stomach ended in a smooth curve which matched the arc of the gel-globe's surface, where it lay contracted in sleep-mode mere inches away.

The rest of the house was empty, and when they had re-gathered from ascertaining this, Trish shot Dr. Winters a look before speaking, and he gave her a nod. "We realized, it dawned on us, that the gel we burned in our lab had, like, consumed a big guy's head and both his hands. It had, like, a shitload of organic material mixed in with it. So . . . what if that was what made it flammable?"

"And if it was," said Dr. Winters, "and tomorrow's attackers are gestating in the bodies of our friends, then tomorrow's new wasps will be vulnerable to fire. Now my friends, for safety's sake, use the hooks, not your hands. Let's see if we can roll it."

What ensued wasn't rolling—it was more like a taffy-pull. The hooks didn't work. They just pulled out tentacles of the gel that shed the points and snapped back into the globe.

They unhinged a small closet door and started working it like a big spatula, forcing the door's edge hard between globe and carpet, heaving up on it like a lever, tipping its mass off balance, and forcing the dense flabby fabric to flop torpidly forward a foot or two, where its sphere re-cohered.

Their sweat drizzled down and their backs ached. When they'd gotten it into the front hall, Cap panted, " 'Nother door!"

Hammering out the pins of a bedroom door, Cap set it long-edge down along one wall: one bank of a channel to guide it out on the porch.

"Now as you lever it up," he grunted, crouching behind the second door and bracing it, "angle it in here so we can squeeze it along between this and the wall."

The gel, once levered into this channel, kept moving in a

V-shaped front, seeking open floor to spread out and re-globe. When it poured out onto the porch, it did just this.

But here it needed only one more levering forward onto the porch steps. Because once the gel was on them, it poured all the way down, rejecting each successive step in its rush for flat ground and sphericity. These it found, and re-formed by the curb.

"Let's find out!" snarled Cap, reaching for Trish's gas rig—which she had to surrender quickly to avoid a bruised shoulder—and leaping down the whole porch-flight in one bound.

They all rushed down after him, and found that the gel, drenched with gas, wore an eerie loveliness. Under its hydrocarbon sheen, lights woke within it—gleams and wisps and nebulae constellated its interior, as if it were a piece of night sky. It looked like the egg of a universe, a *necro*verse of malignant design, and it made more than a few of them think anew that their world had been stolen, and was now in the hands of aliens.

Cap said, "Fire in the hole," and they all stepped back. He thumbnailed a Diamond match alight and flicked it on the sphere.

Then, wearing a crest of whipping flame, the globe seemed a fierce dark eye beneath a blazing brow, while plagues and a whole pox of evils seethed within its gaze. But was it *scathed* in there? Did it just *wear* this fire till shedding it?

". . . Buckling there! The sphere's sagging. . . ."

"Feed it gas! Stand away!"

The gel began to crease in ridges, sag in hollows. "Contraction! Definite!" said Cap—they all stood smiling, watching it, the lumpish and angular subsidence of that baleful star-hive, at last into a coal-black tar, a fuming asteroid half its former mass, jutting in crazy peaks and spiky insect parts.

And not just insect parts. Amid the crooked jumble of protrusions, a slender charcoal stump had sprouted, crowned by part of a human palm, with three crooked fingers.

Out of their stunned silence, Chops growled, grief in his rage, "Oh those murdering motherfuckers."

And then they heard bullhorns up on Glacier Avenue, saw search beams waking sleepers on the sidewalks and porches. The crest-line of the Trinities wore a tiara of silver. The moon was two minutes from rising.

# XX
# A PERFECT CAMEO

**Val stood gazing** at his monitors, the riot of images his scythe of cams harvested from the battle below. He paced as he scanned them, eyes sweeping here and there, the images breathtaking, like a casket of jewels: the town's blazing rivers of battle lights, the sword-blade beams of spotlights swiveling from the roofs of the gun-trucks, the vertical hail of tracers, the shimmery haze of the predators' wings filling the air, and the moon's great scarred, indifferent eye watching from the silvered sky.

But scanned more carefully, the monitors were unsettling.

Those damned swords and shields! What had given them the idea? A few had appeared in the First Act, but now they were everywhere—and were a perfect adaptation to his wasps' mode of attack.

Case in point right there, that punk-haired woman got one's stinger nailed into her shield and twisted it, wrenching the wasp down onto its back, its wings hammering pavement—and there, her burly machete hacking, hacking its head free in two strokes, and the whole monster sagging to gel.

His fingers itched to key his overrides, to dance now this bug, now that one individually was out of danger, but that way lay distraction and futility.

His eye kept gnawing at his strike-count on its screen. If he lost many more APPs to their swords and shields, the strike count was going to be key. Their dead were falling, yes, but would there be enough?

He hated this, seeing his dire, graceful machines captured, damaged, broken. He was becoming aware of an ache that his monitors were starting to give him, an ache in his cheekbone's old fracture.

He touched his face, his fingertips rediscovering for the nth time the flaw inflicted half a lifetime ago.

He had come out of the eroded hulk of Dorsey High's main building, the only part of it that had even half-survived the Zoo's generations of defacement and despoilation. Ten P.M. He came out pumped and happy as he always did from an evening of teaching, his tie loosened, his shirt sweated through that hot July night.

He'd found himself to be a born teacher in those three

years—the ringleader kind of teacher, always on his feet, incessantly bringing his pupils en masse to the board to write what they were learning, and when they were seated, prowling among them as he taught, making each and every one speak solo, with relentless kindness and humor, giving each one his or her moment of limelight and success.

He came out the back of the building, content that he'd reached them, opened a bit more of the world to their eyes—came out, and saw two large shapes standing in front of his motorbike.

There was no moon. Just the Basin's light-haze laying a gray-purple sky on top of the Zoo's shadow-sunk trees and all the ruins nested among them. One of the shapes flipped something into the air—it twirled end-over-end a moment against the sky: a tire iron. This dropped back and was recaptured by the shadow-hand.

He walked up to them without hesitation, still the teacher. "Hey guys. Can I help you?"

"Fuck, no. Give us the bag and empty out your pockets. You can keep your piece-shit bike. We got better."

"You can have my money, but I need the bag. My students—"

And then his face exploded, pavement hammered his back, and his dazed eyes watched the whole sky slowly rocking back and forth. Faraway hands writhed like rats in his pockets. And then there was just silence, and the sky.

There followed a strange and terrible odyssey. First there was rolling over: an endless struggle. Then, sitting up. But standing—this was a desperate war waged against gravity, a war of a hundred reverses, of falling, and rising, and falling again.

When at last he stood, it was a different world he stood in. He saw the Zoo now for the first time. The Zoo had not robbed him. The Zoo had taught him. Had revealed, had explained itself to him. It had taken his money to show him what mattered. It had taken his satchel of books to destroy it, to show him what didn't matter. It had damaged his body to show he was refuse—refused. Teachers couldn't change the Zoo; therefore, they should stay the fuck out of it. The Zoo had fired him: No Teachers Need Apply.

Through that long woozy ride, the pain that had been spiked into his head somehow held him upright. He saw the glow of vid-screens winking from dark windows everywhere. Vid was the only teacher down here, lustful turmoil and gaudy mayhem the only texts, endlessly studied by Zoo-meat while wilderness swallowed their streets. . . .

Val rechecked his strike-count. It was beginning to look like he would make his numbers for tomorrow. He would have scant reserves though, at this pace, might lack the strong backup he liked, to keep them struggling all-out to the very last frame.

His extras—so he still thought of them—redeployed cleverly. Most of the machine-gunners were off the roofs and positioned in second- and third-story windows, weaving a crossfire that was increasingly effective in tearing up APPs as they dropped down into or rose back up from the street. They were actually, here and there, taking their heads off with uncanny aim. Maybe, once tomorrow was secured, he would himself venture a little closer to the action. Enjoy a bit of self-indulgence.

He monitored Mark's and Razz's boats' harrassment of his own. They had some good moves as they scoped his fleet. This was fine because of a recent com received from the Studio's legal division: Panoply would win a suit for ownership of any footage taken of a shoot in progress. Their footage would simply add to the layers of his two-level epic.

He was already filming it from his side too. As Mark's boats rained down like bright flakes, all floodlights and cams, to hang off the bows of Val's boats and harangue them, his boats were camming and haranguing them back, calling them corpse-flies and bootleggers.

He had to smile at Mark's ballsy enterprise. He keyed up one of the harrassments in progress just below him to the north. The enterprising Razz was the haranguer, the counter-haranguer being Trace, one of Val's best pilots.

Razz: "Howzzit feel to watch people die for money?"

Trace: "You mean get paid to kill them, or pay them to die? You should know, you're a fucking director!"

It was beautiful. It would suck the audience into a whole new dimension of involvement, absolve them of their own guilt by making them feel part of a moral inquiry, an exposé.

Why not go lower and tweak things a bit? He called up the feeds from his spray-cams, the freckling of transmission lenses he'd peppered the town with. Excellent for cameo close-ups . . . Hullo. Look at that machine-gunner in that third-floor window there. He was one of that crew that had saved Kate Harlow's ass on *Alien Hunger,* the black kid.

Val was already diving toward the town, when he got a glimpse of another member of that crew—the big white kid. He was gunning from a window on the opposite side of the street.

A perfect window of opportunity.

Val dropped down into the upper stratum of the battle, hung amidst the seethe of wasps rising from one assault and diving to another, pistoning with a silvery hum, striking and soaring. His two chosen extras had very quick reflexes. Val could make this happen. Time for some keyboard work only he could manage.

Their two windows' angles were offset some thirty degrees, the black one's window a few yards higher. Val overrode two APPs now rising to either side of him. His left hand would be for the black extra, his right for the white. Bach himself had done no trickier keying than Val was about to do.

He hovered twelve meters above where the crossfire he meant to create would be flying. His fingers, in two different space-times, brought lefty and righty down to hover at opposite sides of their targets' windows.

Oblivious to Val's control, the gunners swung their muzzles in alignment, each intent only on what hummed and probed not two arm's lengths from his face, not seeing that he was aiming at his ally's window. And . . . action!

Two attacks, perfectly simultaneous, stingers thrust deep within the two windows' frames. But whitey's tracers streamed out an instant before scorching blacky's shoulder with blazing fire. Blacky rolled away from his gun and hugged the floor.

Val probed for him with left wasp's stinger, while feinting with right wasp to keep whitey's fire coming. The man was quick with that machine gun, taking big abdominal chunks out of right wasp. Blacky, still hugging the floor under blistering thirty-cal fire, thrashed as limber as a lizard, ducking both fire and left wasp's thrusts.

These boys were hard to kill.

Val's right hand faltered ever so slightly, and right wasp paused on the downswing for just a beat. Whitey planted a veritable column of hot thirty-cal rounds on rightie, and tore off the lower half of its abdomen. End of crossfire.

And almost in the same instant, blacky flopped and writhed his way back to his machine gun, swung up the barrel, and used it to parry leftie's stinger thrusts, and then poured concentrated fire up into its thorax, holding his target through the wasp's evasions till suddenly the anchorage of one of its wings was shredded, and it fell out of the air.

Val laughed. He had been their Fate, and they had beaten Fate. It happened—it was called heroism, and Val had enabled it, created it. A priceless piece of vid, a perfect cameo. He flagged the footage for the final cut, and began a leisurely vertical ascent.

A massive convergence of thirty-cal fire began hammering on Val's armored underside, like all Hell with jackhammers trying to dig its way up to his ass. His craft must have been recognized—at least a dozen guns were focused on him. He rose a touch higher, and then paused in his ascent, disdaining an undignified evacuation of any part of his set.

Let them hammer away at him a bit, most of their fire was too steep to cross his bows. The state-of-the-art electromag force field rimming his gunwales would deflect the rest.

But, being the very latest thing, and being under increasingly heavy fire, the shield, which micro-instantaneously interpreted and counter-pulsed each impinging projectile's angle of incidence, very briefly glitched.

A sledgehammer blow knocked Val clean out of his seat.

As his eyes slowly cleared, he beheld an otherworldly sphere of light. . . . Realized that he was on his back, staring up at the moon near its zenith.

Vague neural reports began trickling in to him from the outlying regions of his sprawled body. There were his legs . . . his arms. He summoned his right hand. The summons moved slowly through a great inner distance—and after a moment, the hand leadenly raised itself before his eyes. Then, reached down to touch the side of his head. It took a moment for his fingers to report what they touched: hot stickiness. A little more quickly, his head reported receiving this touch: a rusty crack of pain seemed to split it.

The pain was a wakening, and command of his body came with it. He struggled back up to a sitting posture, bent on knowing his damage at once.

Though his head kept swaying out of the vertical, his frame held, and he drew a deep breath. His head was scored, his scalp trenched, his skull maybe grazed, but . . . whole, yes. He commed Medic. "Send me a boat, please, Mirna, I'll need stitches and a cold compress—I'm going straight up to six hundred."

"Roger that, Val."

It was Mirna herself who docked at his portside and came aboard.

"Thanks, dear." Val smiled.

"My god, Val!"

"Not to worry. Just a graze. Some pain med and anti-shock. Dress it carefully please, we don't want too bad a scar."

His own self-possession exhilarated him as much as her medicines, which included forebrain enhancers.

So. He'd survived his second battle wound from the Zoo-meat. His first, long ago, had set him on the path to his present eminence. His second would not unhorse him. He would finish his work here tomorrow, and it would crown that eminence.

And in the process, he would sure as death search out and kill both those fucking extras, white and black.

Val commed his squad chiefs. "That's a wrap, folks. Let's go high, and catch some winks. Tomorrow is a busy day."

# XXI
## BOTTOMS DOWN

**Mark Millar said,** "Damn!"

"Roger that," cried Razz. "Damn!"

Act Three was a wrap. Their rafts hung gunwale to gunwale. They were reviewing their footage of Val near the shoot's end, puppeteering two APPs, almost making two extras kill each other.

"You've gotta admit it," said Razz, still gazing at the display, "that's directing!"

Mark stood up from his console, and paced thoughtfully. Val's near death just made his daring more splendid.

He suddenly felt something cowardly in this high vantage of theirs; that a kind of glass floor was sealing them out of the true mother lode of images.

He realized that Razz stood looking at him from his port side. Razz smiled. "Howdy neighbor. Whatcha thinkin right now?"

"I'm thinking. I'm thinking of getting closer shots of our own."

"Now there's a thought. Because what's the one kind of footage Val won't have? It's street-level footage from a following cam or two."

Mark instantly regretted his words, in which Razz had heard more boldness than he meant. His own thought had been some near-set dives and pullouts. His partner's answer showed him at once the right way to go . . . and how dangerous this was.

Maybe his face betrayed his thought. A little more delicately, Razz said, "It would mean footwork of course. You up for that?"

Mark, eight years the elder, was in great shape and proud of it. And even before his nerves had quite steeled themselves for the venture, he knew that he wouldn't decline what Razz would dare.

"Big Steve and Mike Allen" (their two assistant directors) "can cover Act One in the morning. I think we should be on the ground for that one." Mark felt his nerve catching up with these brave words as he spoke them.

The Third Act had closed on a resounding slaughter of APPs. How would Val field a full force tomorrow? For answer, they had only one vague rumor gathered from insiders at Panoply: the Second Day's assault force of APPs would be a "big surprise."

Both directors carried their own brands of sleep-begone. Mark, resolved now, took a small inhaler from his pocket, and lifted it as in toast to his partner. Razz grinned, and took out his own.

"Bottoms up!" he said.

"Down there," said Mark, "I'm keeping *my bottom down.*"

**"I don't wanna** know—not just yet," Jool said. They were holding each other, side by side on a pew.

Curtis said, "I don't know yet either." They were talking about the number of their casualties.

In the absence of gunfire, it seemed they sat in stillness, though in the streets trucks growled, gathering the dead, and they heard the hoarse, weary shouts of those clearing and repairing their battlements.

In their silence their growing child was with them. Jool hugged him tighter. "You just sleep right here with me now."

"Yes . . ." As carefully as if he was breaking bad news, Curtis said, "But we think we might . . . have something, and they're gonna get me up an hour or so early. I want you to keep sleeping."

"What is it?"

"We think we might be able to burn them after all. The ones tomorrow."

"Why the ones tomorrow?"

"Would you do me a favor? Let me explain after you've had some sleep? Please?"

Jool sighed and let herself settle deeper into him. "Some sleep would be OK," she said. "You know," she said, "when this is over, we got a visit to pay. I mean all of us here. A visit to L.A."

At first Curtis didn't get it. And then he did. He nodded, and they sank in sweet darkness together.

Curtis was stung in the back of the neck. His eyeballs began to swell, grew to big hemispheres that half-covered his head. He had to find Jool, to protect her, but his sight was a mosaic of hundreds of faces that filled the town around him, and he had no other eyes to search this array, to pick out Jool's from the multitude.

He tore them off his face, and had a shotgun in his hands, and there was Jool down the street in a doorway, and the sky was a pavement of monsters at hover just over the rooftops, and he knew that if she stepped out and saw them, the child in her belly would turn to monsters, and he sprinted to reach her, to thrust her back into the doorway—now their house's doorway. He tried to call to her to make her meet his eyes and not look up, but he had no voice.

A hand clutched Curtis's shoulder and he was awake. The sky beyond the broken stained glass was a steely gray. It was Ricky Dawes' hand on his shoulder. The actual world filled back in around Curtis. The world in which his Auntie Drew no longer lived. From which she would be absent for the rest of his life. . . .

"Need you ta help me Curtis—that OK?"

"Sure Ricky—shhhh, let her sleep." He gently disengaged from Jool and followed Ricky out of the church.

"They mostly all gathered," Ricky said as he led Curtis toward the south end of Glacier. Curtis understood that by "they" Ricky meant their dead. "But," he said with a faraway voice, "there's still . . . someone they haven't got yet."

Curtis shot him a look. Said carefully, "You knew him? Or her?"

Ricky shrugged oddly, not meeting his eyes. "Up there, in that alley past Bartlett I think . . ."

The man lay leaned back against the wall at the alley's far end, in a strangely upright posture for a corpse, but one which both men were already used to. So swift was the wasps' poison, the dead often lay strangely poised or propped. There was just enough light now to see that this man's beard was near white.

He was a small corpse that either one of them might have taken alone in a fireman's carry, but the way Ricky took him under the arms from behind told Curtis to take the man's legs and carry him slung between them, which Curtis understood that Ricky meant as an act of respect.

From the moment the two of them were joined face-to-face by this corpse, Curtis knew he must not say a word, that Ricky was struggling to bring out of himself some kind of prayer or testimony for this fallen old fighter (they'd belted a machete that they'd found lying near his dead left hand) and that, not naturally a glib-spoken man, Ricky was trying to find the right words for it. “This here—” It came out in a hoarse bark that startled Curtis slightly. Ricky started again.

“This here old son of a bitch is Hag Barger.” A pause. “This old asshole used to hound me every day of my life since I was, like, eleven! Hootin and brayin at me right out in the street about being an ignore-anus and a school-dodging little retard! Him calling me this! I don’t think he could even read! Or read very much. He’s had me readin the newspaper to him every weekend down at the tavern for I don’t know how long!”

In silence they crossed the street toward the industrial district, while Ricky’s grim face digested yet again this almost lifelong grievance. “There was no place for me to hang out an’ relax in this whole damn town!” he resumed. “He really, like, trammertized my childhood! I mean I’d literally have to go up an’ sit in the hills to have some peace an’ quiet, an’ then sometimes he’d come up past the water tower an’ stand there shouting up the slopes. ‘Hey! Ignore-anus!’ I mean I started to go to school because it was the only place I could get away from him! All this coming from him! He just drank an’ fucked off all day! Grew a little dope and was such a cheat at the scales no one would buy it! The bars didn’t even bother chuckin him out at closing. They just draped a blanket over his head where he sat on his stool, an’ unwrapped him again when they opened!”

In the shadows of the warehouse zone, lay Sunrise’s gathered dead—a strange, long pavement of them, all aligned, all their heads aimed hill-ward, staggered so that the second layer left the chests of the first layer exposed. . . .

When they'd laid Hag down, Curtis found one of his shoes needed retying . . . and then found the other one needed it too, giving Ricky a chance to wipe his eyes on his sleeve unobserved.

Curtis gently thwacked Ricky's gnarled shoulder. "You know what Ricky? We're gonna kill the shit out of these motherfuckers. I mean those ones!"—And he swept his arm at the slice of sky that Panoply's scythe had vacated a few hours before. "I mean the Studio. The next shoot is gonna happen there."

Ricky cleared his throat. "Man, Curtis. You got that sooo right!"

Then, as the pair left the dead, new visitors approached them in a couple of pickups loaded with provisions. These, off-loaded and positioned around the perimeter of the corpses, proved to be machine guns, and spray tanks of gas.

**Mark and Razz** hung low over the slopes a mile up in the hills above town. "I'll take south end," said Mark. "You north?"

"Fine. Meetcha at the water tower—first one hides, second finds him."

Razz slid downslope at half throttle. He loved this terrain-skimming, dipping and winding, the grass tickling his bottom, just hugging the landscape. He was high on this whole derring-do bit, born for it, flowed with it . . . and saw a squat, fast-approaching structure, an outlier of the industrial zone's upslope rim. Keying the raft to tilt, he set it propped on edge, leaning against the upslope wall. Even from one of the town's rafts, it would be tough to spot.

He ghosted now through the grass at a crouch toward the water tank's derrick—would surely beat Mark to it . . . and just as he reached it, noticed a zone of electric lighting in the otherwise dark warehouse zone, mostly hidden by the bulk of a building. Climbing a ways up, he saw some figures approaching that light, and climbing a little more, was just in time to see two men carrying a body before the building obscured them.

A whisper in the grass. "Razz?"

His partner emerged below. Straining to blend their silhouettes with the beams and cross struts, they climbed the tank's supports till they could just make out a machine gun on a tripod flanking the lighted zone, and someone manning it.

The two traded a long look. "Maybe they heard some rumor we didn't," said Razz.

"Yeah. I have a feeling that down there is just where we want to be camming, come sunrise."

A short silence followed. "It won't be easy," said Razz, "finding cover down there. All that open space."

". . . And we want it between us, want to get crosswise angles on it."

"We'd better get started before it gets lighter."

# TICKING DOWN

**Gillian opened her** eyes. In the void where the Virgin's head had been was gray sky, and the raft-scythe was already aloft there, waiting for sunup. She looked down at Jool, asleep at her side.

Gillian had grown up on rezzes in three different states. And now she had a second dear friend from L.A., this second friend once her first friend's lover. She touched Jool's cheek, smiling with the new thing she'd learned: when you've saved someone's life, you love them.

Jool's eyes came open, as if she'd heard her thought.

Their gazes caught and mingled, sharing an unspoken hope that they might get to live as friends, as sisters. Gillian said, "It's near time. We should get everyone up."

"First I have to pee. Both of me have to pee."

"Me too."

The church had a two-stall ladies' room. Jool said through the partition, "You know, I'm clumsier, but I think she makes my mind clearer. Like she helps me think."

"So you think she's a she."

"I just know she's a she."

As they washed their hands and faces, Jool added, "It's like I feel her warning me—to your right . . . behind you—like her thoughts coming right up my wiring. Like she's got my back in there."

"Got your back and a lot of the rest of you too." They laughed. Gillian gave her a hug. "You're tough." She smiled.

"So are you."

"Yeah. I can fight. But you're like . . . an antibody. All those streets you've traveled growing up, colliding with other corpuscles, fighting what came along."

"So I'm round, like a corpuscle."

"A tough corpuscle."

They went back out, still laughing, and began to wake the others, getting the youngest and oldest to the bathrooms first. . . .

**Mark Millar, though** just a bit terrified, exulted. He was on the roof of a building that neighbored the larger one along which the dead were laid. It had a slightly sloped roof with a parapet around it. He lay snugged in the parapet's corner, his cam snaked down and out through its drain port. The corner would shadow him when the sun emerged. He wasn't invisible, but pretty damn close, at least till the sun moved overhead. His cam showed him a breathtaking field of potential action.

In the arc lights surrounding them, the dead looked composed. Visible wounds were few. The scuffs and scrapes of vigorous battle marked them here and there, but their calm was absolute. Naked faces and limbs embroidered the array with flesh. This flesh seemed surreally solid, looked like a pavement of dense matter as old as the mountains. In their solidity, in the staggered pattern of their stacking, these dead looked like the first-laid length of a funereal highway that might climb to the peaks of the Trinities.

In a broader ring surrounding the arc lights, the crude machinery of self-defense was deployed. Here was epitomized the eternal human struggle with death: blunt hammers arrayed to strike down that dark angel so inhumanly swift.

Twenty machine guns were arrayed in a crescent along the outer rim, their muzzles exquisitely aligned to keep the flow of fire pouring lengthwise up the dead array, avoiding both ricochet from the wall, and mutual damage. Flanking each gun on the right was a fire team: a guy with a tank-and-nozzle and a flare-gunner to ignite the gas.

Why would these people vandalize even further that unearthly pavement of their kin and friends? Then he realized that somehow they'd learned it was from their dead that today's new death would come.

Mark's gift had always been to grasp Val's genius, and he acknowledged it now. Great art must be implacable, and Val was great, he granted this. But he also thought, and not for the first time, that this was a vile kind of greatness. Was Mark, rising master of Live Action, rooting for the extras now? He was.

But would he lay by the crown that his work here would win him? Abandon Live Action forever? No way.

Aiming his lens across the yard, he zoomed on the rear of a three-story house. It was dormered, and in the lower corner of the dormer's window frame he found the little glint of Razz's fiber-optic winking back at him. Whatever happened here would be captured between them.

Mark felt a faint prickle of anti-grav along his back. Two steel circles bit against the nape of his neck.

"As I live and breathe!" A woman's voice that he knew. A merry voice. "It's Mark Millar! Vid-wizard extr'ordinaire!"

It amazed Mark, how huge those two steel holes felt, pressed against his neck. Endless space in them, two tubular voids where his whole life could vanish in a tick.

Soon after, in her raft, Sharon Harms sat enjoying the sight of him. Mark was seated as she was, but shackled to his chair. Her cornflower eyes and freckles somehow made her sweet smile scary. "First things first, Mark. Let's go get your raft."

**Around the gunners** that flanked the dead we set up an outer machine-gun ring to get anything that got up past them. The sun when it came would hit us in the eyes. Less than fifteen minutes left . . .

Four rafts set down on the yard behind us. Two were ours, loaded with weapons. The other two were sleeker and more high-tech looking. Our rafters began installing guns in these sportier boats.

Sharon Harms flew out over the lot, and in her cheerful, neighborly way told us the news—telling it to our dead as well it seemed, who lay waiting among us to wage a second day of war.

"Two new fighters in our fleet—slick boats too! Sandy and I'll be flyin 'em. That high fleet there stealing Val's shoot? The one he sent up his APPs to kill? We got both their directors' boats and one a their directors himself! We got their shoot's master-cams! We own their fucking vid of Margolian shooting us! Makes your head swim, don't it? We got a real stake in this flick now, folks!"

That got some bleak laughter out of all of us. "Serious now!" Sharon cried. "Bo-koo clacks to be had off this flick of our flick. So. I told you we got just one a their directors but both of their rafts. Whaddya think? You think that other director's down here too?" Sharon cocked a yoo-hoo hand to the side of her mouth and called louder: "Hey! Mr. Razz-matazz! Pretty close by, are you? Don't make us shoot you. We just wanna give you a job. We want you running the cams on your boat for us! We all get rich together!"

That got a cheer from us, but we were feeling the clock. Twelve minutes left. Things got busy around the new rafts.

Guns were being mounted, pilots being given a crash course at the consoles by our shackled captive. And now, high above Panoply's scythe, came that smaller, thinner crescent of raft-bottoms: the vid-thieves. Our vid-thieves now.

Others converged round our dead. Devlin's boat arrived, and a little after, some skinny kid rode in slow on a rumbling Harley.

And a few beats later, Devlin half-shouted, "How else you think we fight, fool?"

I could see now that the kid on the bike was a young woman. "All due respect," she piped, "screw you too! Just getting clear, here: you give me that boat, it's mine."

Devlin laughed, an angry laugh, but she seemed to enjoy this kid too. "Girl, that's a given." And now she shouted to all the rafters, "Let's all get crewed and mount up. Zero minus eleven minutes!"

I could feel us all thinking it, and so I shouted it out: "If we got even a piece of the take on this bootleg vid of theirs, we could bring a fucking army down on Panoply!"

That set everyone talking. No one dared turn from their guns or their gas, because they all knew what was shortly to erupt from the heaped corpses before them, but everyone was shouting some hope and some heart back and forth.

But hope's double-edged. Start craving that future, and you really start feeling the knife at your throat here and now. I had to see Jool once more, had to hold her again before the shit hit the fan. I signaled to the others, and booked it for the church.

Everyone there was at the ready—youngest and oldest hunkered down in the pews, gunners stationed at the doors, in the aisles. Jool stood center-aisle front. She had to be quick setting her Thompson aside, so urgent I was to get my arms around her.

"Not so hard you sweet fool, you'll crush baby."

"Jool. Listen. Don't . . . Don't."

There was no way to say it. I remembered the first time I saw her, standing by her book racks on the freeway off-ramp. Here she was, mine now. Her stern little Mexican/Indian don't-fuck-with-me face. I wanted to tell her not to die, but couldn't bring that word out between us.

But she got it, and took my face in her hands. "I won't—we won't. Don't you either. Don't you dare."

We stood holding each other, and I looked around us. The stained-glass window's whole top third was gone—just the fragment of a child left, lying on his mother's lap. I looked at all these women and children around us. I couldn't believe what was happening to us. These were *people.* To use them for props, for targets in a kill-fest! It seemed like something only an alien could do, some bug from Altair in a cheesy sci-fi. And there they were. Out past the headless Mother, their rafts paved the sky.

I told Jool about the captured directors' boats. It seemed cold comfort as I said it, but the mad light it put in her eyes warmed me.

"We own the vid? You know what we could do with that kind of money?"

"Yes. Annihilate Panoply."

She kissed me. "Go on back to work now, dear. Baby needs a new pair of shoes."

**Sunrise's fleet cycled** through the town's airspace, and Sandy had just bullhorned "shoot minus five" to the town at large. Mazy, without tailing her outright, was keeping Ming's raft in range, a little miffed that her hothead lover had scored a flashier raft than hers. She laughed at herself for it, but being an ace pilot in her own right, was still a bit ticked.

Ming held at hover. She seemed to be looking down into the trees on the downslope side of town. When she flew down toward them, Mazy was already slanting to intercept her.

"Whatcha got?"

"I think I saw movement. Yes. Look there, two thirds up in that pine."

They slowed coming in, their hesitation growing as they neared a dull, glossy bulk that cleaved to the trunk.

"Is that . . ." Ming asked, ". . . a wasp?"

It might have been, if a wasp had folded its abdomen up against its thorax, and wrapped itself with its wings into a glossy-crusted, obese cocoon.

"Not anymore I don't think," said Mazy. "It's like . . . changing into something else."

The cocoon crinkled slightly, crumpled a little, and then swelled out again. "That's what I saw," said Ming. "That fucker's gonna go active."

As she opened up her machine gun on it, Mazy commed Sandy. "We got an APP cocooned in a tree. Looks active. We need to scope all the trees."

**In the little** dormered room overlooking all the town's guarded dead, Razz was crouched low. Down on the ground floor, the front door banged open and he heard people trooping in.

He scuttled to the side window, leaned out and gripped a sturdy downspout. Took a deep breath, and swung himself outside, hugging the wall as he did it. He managed to get his foot on the top of the masonry frame of a first-floor side window, and to push his hand up against the bottom frame of the second-story window directly above it.

With his back flat to the wall, isometrically clamped between the heels of his upthrust hands and the soles of his feet, Razz considered his position. In shape as he was, he was OK for a couple minutes, but then he would start feeling crucified. At his back and beneath him he heard people come into the room whose window frame he stood on. Down beneath his footsoles a head thrust out, looking up and down the alley that flanked the building, then pulled back inside without looking overhead.

Razz was stuck, as on flypaper, to one wall of a set. A live-action set. It led him to a kind of epiphany. All these people here were stuck, as on flypaper, to a live-action set. Why didn't they all just clear the fuck out of here, head for the hills? Anything but this! And then Razz remembered that pavement of dead he'd just been camming. Whatever had kept them here fighting yesterday, what kept them here now were all their fallen.

Now up in the room he'd just left were voices and movement. If he had to jump and bolt, where could he go? On the opposite side of the alley, there was a low slot of shadow in the base of the wall—an entry port to an under-floor crawl space. He reminded himself this wasn't a set but a real town, full of odd nooks and coverts . . . He heard clear speech from the dormered room above:

". . . our posts—it's minus five."

Don't think. He jumped, arms spread for balance. His legs just took the shock, though he toppled forward and badly bruised his knee. Then he rolled, and scuttled into the crawl space.

Gasping, he lay easier in darkness, in the cool smell of earth and old floor beams. Safe. Or pretty damned likely to be, down here out of the view of death on wings. He heard fast footfalls out in the alley, and recoiled from the parallelogram of light coming in through the slot, worming deeper into the dark. One . . . two pairs of track shoes jogged past the slot.

Razz sighed his relief, spread his arms to assume a more comfortable prone posture, and felt his right forearm make contact with a weighty, slightly resilient mass.

His whole body contracted and he crab-scrambled sideways—lay straining his eyes into the dark, and after endless seconds began to discern the dimly lit floor beams and, just under the nearest one, a glossy, globular blackness, perhaps half again the diameter of a large beach ball.

No need to bolt—not yet. A mass of gel, in dormant mode. It wouldn't move, not till the shoot started. But he'd have to bolt soon, find another hide. The size of that thing! It must have consumed . . . half a man anyway. Or pieces of several men, or women . . . ?

Razz had thought he'd confronted what he did for a living—for a small fortune, actually. He thought that he had taken a square, manly look at it, had faced its grim realities and made his peace with them. But he, his industry, was creating these things. These wizardly machines that devoured human flesh! Had his job devoured his mind? Making things like these was not a sane thing to do!

And then he heard a noise that turned his whole body to stone. Machine-gun fire—its roar rising as gun after gun joined the chorus, a massive barrage awakening down just west of town. The shoot had started!

Razz remembered how fast—once activated—the gel could flow, and his muscles were suddenly spring-steel. He launched sideways, and rolled hard for the entry-slot.

He came flopping out into the alley and got his legs under him, and sprinted for Main Street. The shit-storm was raging and he had to get armed at once. He was in the fight now, and had to find allies but fast.

He burst out of the alley mouth, found a heavily armed young woman posted right beside it and shouted, "I lost my gun! Gimme a weapon!"

A slow smile spread on her face. "Hey!" she said brightly. "You must be the other director."

While she spoke, Razz was realizing something. Glacier

Avenue was full of fighters, all down along both sidewalks, and its forces were fully mobilized, pickups and battle-vans slowly cruising in both directions, and all the second-floor windows had thirty-cal muzzles jutting from them—but no one was firing! And there were no APPs in sight!

The young soldier cupped a hand to her mouth and called, "Arms!" and a pickup slid to the curb. The guy in the bed gave her a cut-down twelve-gauge, an ammo pouch, and a shield. She gave Razz the shield first. "Wear it on your left with the left hand free enough to work the slide." She gave him the sawed-off. "You cover that alley from here. Watch my back, and I'll watch yours." Her sudden grin came back. "Less than shoot minus three now, pilgrim! And counting. . . ."

# XXIII
# PREMATURE EXECUTION

**Machine-gun barrages, stitching** the pine trees below town. The tracers of converging fire from half a dozen rafts etched a sudden geometry of acute angles, all focused in the trees where near a hundred of his APP survivors clung cocooned. It was still shoot minus four!

Val flinched as if from a slap in the face. He ached for vengeance . . . and almost laughed. What greater hurt than all of this could he inflict on them?

His head wound throbbed. He fought for calm. Sit

absolutely still. One heartbeat . . . two . . . three. He must not lose control.

Control was hard to manage, because Val had been so angry already. Had watched, with dawning disbelief, as the Sunrisers assembled round their dead, and enfiladed them with focused fire power.

A leak . . . Or perhaps not a leak. Val willed himself to unclench. Someone down there had known about oviposition. This was a big community—how hard was it to guess that someone here might know? Had he really thought them all hicks because they lived in the mountains? In our pride, he thought, we dumb down our enemies.

And they were by-god nailing him for it now. It was his art that they were scrambling in those cocoons, just as it had been his flesh, his face they had cracked with their tire iron so long ago. He saw it clearly for the first time, this simple, glaring truth. Those dire, gorgeous anatomies gestating there were his art and thus himself, and every one of them a killer pure and simple.

Well . . . fair enough. Or true enough. But what then? Each man has his own script he must live, if he chooses to create something, and not simply to follow the throng. And except for this shoot, except for this one time, Val's career had been blameless. He had set up his booth in the open market, and offered possible death for major cash—and the takers had come, filling the sets.

And below him, on his screens right now, was the proof that he ran an honest casino. Those extras were raking in his chips down there! He'd fucked up somehow, and right from the starting gun these Sunrisers were shredding his APPs and kicking his ass.

Those crushed in the mine—how he felt their loss now! These raft-gunning bitches raking the trees were sharp-eyed. They were punching his tickets left and right as he watched. Be still, heart!

He drew a deep cleansing breath. Another. He must be cold, take counsel with himself and bide his time. He must not jump the clock by even a second. React to their lawlessness, and he'd break his inner rhythm. The extras then would set the tempo, and he would stay half a beat behind them thereafter.

That would be to repeat his near-fatal error on *Alien Hunger*. There, by plunging into his shoot, he'd come within an ace of being devoured by his own APPs while it was all recorded by his own cams! And memory's cams starkly replayed for him the eyes of that huge spider, the cringing of his own flesh as its fangs so nearly pierced him.

Recalling this chastened his anger, and chilled his blood.

And in this new calm, he saw how he could indulge himself in just one tidbit of revenge. He set his fingers flying on APP uplinks . . . and swiftly isolated just the one he wanted out of his hundreds: one cocoon so well hidden in pine boughs that none of the raft gunners had seen it, though no less than three of them were deployed in positions not six yards from it.

Even as he watched the carnage worked on a score of his

other cocoons—a spill of garbled bodies, of shredded limbs and smashed heads spraying in clots from their torn pupae—he accelerated to perfect form the hidden one at the gunners' backs.

Even as the nearest gunner—a lean young woman—whipped round her gun toward the sound of its fractured chrysalis, its great height overtopped her, dire arms lanced toward her, and razor jaws bit off her head.

The APP instantly gave him a tight zoom on its prey's avenger—a second lean young woman, her face all wrath and horror, obliterating the APP's head and eyes, and the shot itself.

More calmly now, Val accepted the carnage amidst the pines—twenty-six cocoons already savaged. Just watch them at their work—most of them rafters from Panoply itself.

And then Val realized that their fleet was larger since yesterday—was . . . eleven rafts strong! There was the big sector-boat, the eight fast-rafts he knew . . . and two more fast-rafts, slightly bigger, more powerful models. Director's rafts.

He commed one of his assistant directors. "Harvey? Give me an exact count of Shoot Two's fleet. See if they're short." He'd appropriated Mark's pirate work above them as "Shoot Two," an addition to their own.

He waited, weighing the possibility that Mark and Razz had joined the Sunrisers. It would give them footage from the extras' POV—priceless stuff! But meaning, he reminded himself, that would give him that footage.

"They're short two rafts, Val."

"Thanks Harv. Feed me an overhead zoom on those two directors' boats gunning the trees."

"Roger that."

And on the zoom, Val instantly recognized one of the pilots: that little cornflower skag, Sharon Harms—an ace Panoply payboater and notorious hot dog. A wave of dread rose in him. Though they might collude with the Sunrisers, neither Mark nor Razz would willingly put his boat in an extra's control. . . .

He scanned his feeds of Glacier Avenue, a dire premonition upon him. An odd little cameo on the sidewalk drew his eye: a truck pulling to the curb, and a man—apparently still unarmed at this late hour—being handed weapons from its bed. Val zoomed in.

There he was. Razz. Assuming arms and taking up a post at an alley mouth.

Now Val could no longer resist understanding: the extras owned Millar's whole meta-vid. They had captured its master-rafts! The two directors' rafts were the automatic ultimate repository of their whole fleet's shoot.

Val's legal control of that footage made no difference anymore. The extras would bootleg it into the market for a fucking mint.

That would only sharpen the market for Val's own vid, of course, and make him a mint of his own, but that didn't matter. That didn't help at all. The Studio, he, would be trumped. *Assault on Sunrise* would be stolen, stolen *by*

Sunrise, and sold by Sunrise under its own imprimatur to all the wide vid-sucking world!

And as bad as this—*worse* than this, really—they had robbed him of a priceless scene, one he'd been savoring since he'd first finished scripting this opus.

Day Two, Act One, Scene One. Just minutes from now it would have unfolded: the second generation of APPs swarming up from the trees, and raining down on the rooftops. The Sunrisers took arms and ran to battle, heartened to face a foe much reduced.

And this scene's POV was from the heap of gathered dead, from eyes that emerged from those dead. Just the tops of their heads emerged, faceted spheres that covertly erupted from the midriffs and ribs of the fallen.

Jewels, those eyes—sprouting like toadstools all over that funeral pile. Slowly they swelled, their wraparound vision capturing one another's emergence, capturing the whole unsuspecting town in fractured-rainbow radiance. . . .

A pull-back shot of the heap then: whole heads sprouting everywhere, their dire jaws gaping, while all the dead grew restless, all trembling, twitching, shrinking slightly—as if they dreamed what was happening to them.

And only then would his demons tear free and take to the air.

Grim now, Val waited for what he must do. Let the sun rise. . . .

**Mark Millar sat** snugly—all too snugly—in a crew chair just aft of Sandy Devlin. She was nosing their raft—

Mark's raft—to port and starboard, swaying like a cobra's head, searching the trunks of the trees for cocoons.

Mark, himself cocooned in duct tape to his chair, said, "Sandy. Listen. These two boats of mine have cams. As long as you're flying them, would you please just have those cams on?"

She let out a caw of derision. "Why do you think I've got you aboard?"

"Wonderful!" And Mark meant it; he could see now he was going to survive this. "Here it is," he urged her. "The whole can of worms. You've got us, and we know you'd hurt us if we forced the issue. The thing is, you need us to edit and package and market the vid. We'll give you twenty-five percent of the gross."

Sandy laughed. Her eyes never left their search of the trees as she answered. "Oh Mark, you devil! Don't you know your asses aren't leaving our hands till you've deeded our clacks to us? We won't skin you as bare as we could. You get thirty-three percent when our sixty-six is banked, and you two get codirectors' credit along with Sunrise, Inc., but our name comes first."

"We have to—"

"Nope. All that, or you fall out of this raft from three hundred feet, and we print and market the vid ourselves."

"Sandy!" It was the yelp of a wounded puppy, but Sandy sensed compliance waiting in the wings, after a little more pummeling.

"And think on this, Mark," she said. "There's gonna be a sequel. If you do a great job here, we're gonna let you shoot it, and for half the gross." Still she watched the trees, but she could feel that word "sequel" banging around in Mark's mind. And then could feel him getting it.

"All-righty then," she said, "it's shoot minus forty seconds." She spun round to face him, reaching the razor beak of a utility knife toward him. She sliced just his forearms free, so he could manipulate the console. "Got enough flexibility there, Mark?"

"I can make it work, thanks." He was keying a sharp, sweet zoom on a cocoon that a rafter was shredding with thirty-cal fire.

"Hey Millar," said Radner. Sandy had him tail-gunning, always flew with him. He was a small, nervous guy, as well balanced as a monkey—as he had need to be, with Devlin driving. "Can you cam me too? Get some shots of my gunning?"

"I'm already doing it, Rad," Mark said pleasantly.

**At shoot minus** zero, as the sun lit shafts of flame on the crests, every cam raft in the sky, in both the smaller and the greater scythes, was sucking photons from the same spot: that funerary pavement of the dead, with all those Sunrise guns—powerless to save their lives—now trained just above their corpses.

And through these corpses, movement rippled, and through the nerves of all those eyes-in-the-sky as well it rippled, as awe, and commiseration, and a cruel delight in power a-borning.

Barbed bug legs erupted like a forest of thorn trees, tearing a passage for huge fanged heads. Sprays of cold blood and torn flesh celebrated their birth like flung confetti. Shreds of tissue bearding the thorns, those crooked trees clawed at the sky, seemed to find purchase on the air that hauled them higher into view. Long bodies—limber shafts—thrust up and wide green wings scissored open, became bright, buzzing blurs in the sunlight that lifted—more powerfully now—long abdomens, long, trailing legs toward the sky.

And all this sudden crop of gorgeous demons, so furiously alive, was reaped as it rose by a sleet of machine-gun fire.

In this zone their substance sprayed through the air, became an aerial stratum of wheeling fragments, barbed graspers sailing like flung boomerangs, eyes streaking like meteors and flashing like rainbows, wing-shards wheeling away like crystal blades . . . And amidst this carnival of vengeance, there were festival blazes everywhere, little bonfires that writhed and clawed for the air as they blazed and sank, wings crisping. Ignited, these brutes burned, and shrank to cinder!

But their number was twice the dead that housed them. They rose in such a fire-absorbing locust storm that near two hundred flew unscathed above that web of fire, hung like scythe-armed angels against the sky, gem-eyed executors of an alien deity's will. Dangling abdomens sleek-lined like war canoes. The legs their thorax trailed—two pair—long too, and strongly jointed, promising lethal leverage for the brutal forelegs—these made not for standing, but only to seize.

A greenish iridescence was their color, and they blazed with sentience. Much bigger-headed than their models the mantids, their hemispheric eyes deployed a spherical surveillance. Nothing could elude them, and their fanged jaws declared their appetite for every biped gazing up at them.

The two fleets hung in wonder, every eye devouring these devourers. Until . . . a thousand eyes zoomed quick on their first kill: a roof-gunner seized from behind in two barbed V's, triangular jaws engulfing the man's head from behind, and biting it clean off.

And the Sunrisers had seen more than this. Had seen, as the bug alighted on the gray slate roof for its kill, how its whole body—even its eyes—had turned the same slate-gray, so that the roof-gunner had almost seemed seized by the air itself. But once its prey was seized, the bug resumed its own hue, a demon exquisitely distinct engulfing the head, biting it off, and letting fall the fountaining stump.

**"Whoa!" said Mike** Allen to Big Steve. They rode gunnel to gunnel, feeding off their screens, Mark and Razz's two Assistant-Directors-Now-In-Charge. "Day Two! Val's the Dark Wizard Himself, isn't he?"

"Truth! That man is deeply deranged!"

"Whaddya mean? This is much more humane than those fuckin spiders! Think I better com Mark? His raft, I mean?"

They had Mark too on zoom—or Mark's head, atop a silvery mummy of duct tape. Big Steve nodded and Mike commed: "Sandy? Hi. Is it OK to speak to Mark?"

"Hi Mike! Here he is."

"Hi Mark. Should we, uh, continue uplink to you?"

"That's a most definite affirmative, Mike. No uplink from us, though. We have a new partner. Not to worry, we all get paid, that's guaranteed."

"Roger that, Mark. Back to work."

Mike Allen clicked off. Both he and Big Steve were still rapt by their screens.

The nasty new thing about these bugs was, they didn't stay airborne long. They dove right onto and into the set. They hit rooftops and walls and ran nimbly across both with equal ease, even along the undersides of overhangs. And since they nearly vanished the instant they landed, it was only stray flashes, just a sketch of their shapes the defenders saw scattering everywhere. It was an uncanny adaptation. Even when they crossed an optical border—from concrete to asphalted roofing, from shadow to sunlight—their disguise was instantly bipartite, their foreparts matching what they entered, their hindquarters what they were leaving.

But when they struck and fed, and whenever they leapt through the air, you saw them whole—they were plunging into Glacier Avenue all down its length. Windows were exploding inward, the mantids crowding inside unharmed by the shards—clearly designed for inside work as well, to scour out the refuges that had sheltered and saved so many extras yesterday.

The mantids hatched from cocoons—scores of them surviving the air-gunning—joined the fray, flooding up from the trees below town, and melting into Sunrise's lower rim.

And all over town now, they harvested human defenders.

The grip of their forelimbs was brusque and as absolute as heavy machinery, and as their color came clear, you saw how the men who thrashed in their grip could not shake their mechanized strength, till quick decapitation froze their struggles, and they were dropped, lax as dolls.

Mike shouted, "Just look how they're burning!" Fire teams had run into the streets now—gas drenched the invaders and hissing flare guns lit them up. As the wasps had done yesterday, they clenched and contracted in flight . . . but this generation could not snuff out their cremation. Their limbs contorted and crisped, wings buckled, and they crashed to earth to lie there ablaze.

**Val watched on** his screen the tape-silvered Mark Millar keyboarding the cam board of his own raft. Envy ate at him. Val's peppering of imbedded lenses couldn't give him mobile in-fight footage like this. Those two directors' boats down there were scooping him.

With their aerial footage and this in-battle stuff, the traitors had the whole solid geometry of his shoot in their hands; had an epic that would enclose his own like a clamshell, Val's art itself captured from beneath and above.

His footage of course was the pearl in the shell, the narrative that would make their meta-shoot matter at all. He, Panoply, would be immensely enriched. But the fortune they would pocket, the extras! And with Mark's connivance their meta-vid would be professionally edited, acquired by some dummy corp to which their names had no connection.

Two junior directors sharking for rep and for power—

and they would gain both. They need only put the word of this vid on the streets in L.A. and backers would besiege them with giga-clacks. Sunrise would surely cut them serious cash, and with their Zoo connections would know just how to run it past the law and into the market.

Grimly, resolved now to face a stark assessment, Val unwound the last tentacle of surveillance that had enfolded him. Mark's cams had surely seized on Val's dive last night into his seething creation, caught his orchestration of wasps and machine-gun fire, his stately retreat, and then his wounding, his own body flung slack and bloody in its throne.

The appalling intimacy of this possession! His own near-death.

But as outrage flared in him, his director's eye was . . . dazzled. When all was said and done, what a scene!

The director himself, wounded in action, himself risking death for his art! How it was edited would be key: his resolute entry of the fire zone, his dispassionate artistry with his two winged executioners, his thoughtful, unhurried reascension—and then his head wound, his laying low. His death itself it would seem to be at first, so close it had been.

Almost, he resolved to deploy cam boats of his own down closer to rooftop level.

No. Again that temptation to yield the initiative, and thus yield control. *Hang tough, and wait.*

He gazed at his zoom of Mark, stiffly keying away down there. If Val had those two rafts—had just one of them—he would have everything.

He commed Aidan Zadok, his Properties chief, and

they talked about their APPs' flight-speed maximum in short bursts. The mantids were clumsier than his wonderful wasps—foot soldiers more than airborne. They were *devourers.* To catch and eat weighty prey like men, they had to have mass, leverage.

His chat with Properties brought him solace. Yes, flight-speed might be an issue, but on balance, his props chief thought that, from rooftops, the mantids might very well be gotten aboard low-flying rafts.

# COMBAT

**They invaded Glacier** Avenue. It wasn't the pavements they swarmed, but the walls—they came in little squadrons running slantwise across the fronts of buildings, little arrowheads and dagger-blades of half a dozen mantids, scuttling in perfect synchrony zig and zag over verticals of plaster, carpentry, and concrete.

"Look at that!" barked Chops—and Cap could only nod. Chops meant an arrow of them darting from a brick façade and down across gray stucco. As they crossed the juncture their foreparts grayed, hindquarters brick-red till they crossed the instant after.

Their rippling camouflage was everywhere, pausing at windows and balconies, testing them, and here and there breaking through and pouring inside.

"They're after refuges!" Cap shouted to the street—"They want max kills!"—as he and Chops were sprinting to intercept a squad slanting down the face of the three-story Traveller's Rest. Cap came under them, shield hoisted on his left, his up-stretched right unleashing double-ought ammo that just missed, spraying off a gout of abdomen, chambered a second while still running and found his aim, tearing a hind leg out from under the bug.

One instant it faltered and the next it leapt off the wall, resuming its own color then, its wings unscissoring with a greenish flash to steer its swift dive straight on Cap.

He twisted his bulk down tight into his shield-shadow. The beast's full weight pressed down, the graspers bit wood at both sides, the spiked tip of the left gashing his forearm deep, as its jeweled eyes and fangs thrust near Cap's face and chawed at the air.

So intimate with the monster's mass was he, Cap felt through his shoulder Chops's shotgun blast, the concussion of its double-ought with the brute's left grasper at the shoulder.

It sagged away to gel as Cap heaved his own strength up and outward against the bug's half-grip on him, a grip it could not free from the soft wood that had snagged it. The mantid's missing rear leg told—its center of gravity shifted sideward and it was torqued nearly to the ground. In this brief contest Chops found time to circle round behind and blow the mantid's head off and to gel.

The APP did not for an instant cease to press its grim strength contrary to Cap's muscle-cracking labor to pin it down. "Its other arm!" he bellowed, "Then it's got nothing!"

But Chops was already doing it: Whack! *Slick-click* Whack!

And with that arm blown free, not only it but the whole mantid deflated to gel.

"Those skanky fuckers!" Cap raged. "The trigger's both arms!"

They saw the street was now full of struggle. The wall-swarms had come leaking everywhere down onto the ground, were asphalt and concrete in color, but now there was no mistaking seven-foot eye-level monsters. It was full engagement, and everyone had to know now.

"Both their arms!" Cap bellowed to the town. "Take off both their arms!"

He knew his end one pulse before it came—a swift deployment of mass above and behind him. Barbs sank into his shoulders and his chest, hoisting him up and back into the jaws. A demon's head with rainbow eyes engulfed his own, and closed the book of his kindness and courage forever.

Everywhere shield and sword teams had brutes down, barbs locked on shields, and with a frenzied diligence were hacking at every part of them. Headless thoraxes, half their legs gone, dragged sword teams in circles as our people hacked at any piece of the homicidal amputees they could reach.

But word spread, and after a timeless fury, a fugue of dark, adrenalized toil, new danger underfoot was everywhere, because bugs were collapsing wholesale to globes and big tongues of questing gel.

But then the bugs had flowed up to the walls again, resumed their evasive flow, their searching for entry into buildings. A lull had come to the attack down in the street. Chops, wiping his eyes, dragged Cap off the street and wrapped him in a tarp. The palm of his hand still stung with the stars Cap had put there. He laid it on the dead man's chest, a good-bye and a promise of vengeance.

More than a dozen headless souls lay bleeding along the street, like toppled amphorae spilling their contents. People were grieving, were torching gel, were howling curses at the sky. Chops worked his way down the length of the street, shouting the message on Cap's lips when he died. "Blow their arms off! Both their fucking arms!"

**The battle plan** was spreading everywhere. "Reinforce refuges and get more armed defenders inside them. The bugs are only feinting in the streets, and going for maximum kills in refuges. And don't waste shot on anything but their arms."

Japh shouldered his gun—not too hot. The attack up here had been suspiciously thin—caught up a case of ammo belts, and got himself down into the street. Saw a guy he could use. "Ricky! Stop that truck and get a thirty! I need your help!"

He and Dawes jogged down the sidewalk weightily armed. "The Majestic's harboring hundreds. Its entries need more cover. I'll guard the front. I think you need to guard the back too."

They jogged into the alley behind the theater. A Z of

metal stairs climbed the back wall to the projection floor, reached through an ordinary door, not strong—and all the more obviously so as two mantids were well along in tearing it down.

"Cheap fuckin fiber-wood door!" shouted Ricky. "We gotta shotgun 'em. Thirties'll fly on into the theater!"

Setting down their big guns they sprinted up the stairs drawing their sawed-offs. They stopped three risers below the brutes and opened fire on them. Chunks of their graspers went flying, but these parts' quickness made them damnably hard to hit. One's head came off, jounced past them down the stairs unregarded. Both mantids persisted in tearing at the doors until the double-ought's damage commanded their attention.

They turned in counterattack. Then their graspers, outreached from above, made better targets. A half-dozen fusillades and they'd whittled them down to the shoulder-stubs.

An avalanche of gel poured down the stairs, and they were in.

The door was little more than a rag of wood fiber. They unhinged it and threw it aside, lay a big metal desk on its side and blocked the lower half of the doorway. Ricky mounted his thirty behind it.

"Cut 'em off at the waist," Japh called, bounding back down the stairs, "and their arms can't reach ya! *Then*, take their arms off."

Ricky went inside, down a short hall past the projection booth to a little balcony above the theater itself, where projectionists had once enjoyed their movies from an armchair.

He looked down from there at his neighbors in their cavernous refuge.

A sea of anxious eyes met his gaze. He gave them an awkward little wave, and got relieved waves in return. "Not to worry folks," he called. "We got your backs up here."

Japh found covering the theater's front doors trickier. It had a shallow, plain atrium, where the box office and posters once were, then, just beyond a sketch of a lobby, the four old-fashioned swinging doors that opened with push bars straight into the theater. These bugs could hammer right through them.

He seriously needed more guns with him here. He set his thirty at the left of the doors to fire out at the incoming where they funneled into the atrium. Then he scanned the buildings directly across the street, figuring the angle of his gun's elevation so his fire would hit only sky.

Dr. Winters and Trish jogged into the atrium. Winters, recognizing in Japh a young man he knew for a reader, immediately unburdened himself. "It's ludicrous! These things are Mantidae! They're not even of the same order as wasps!"

And, as if doing it only to express his anger at this phylogenetic outrage, when a mantis came sprinting toward them, he fired his twelve with a scowling, deliberate expertise that pleasantly surprised Japh—and blew one of its graspers off.

**The banquet room** on the ground floor of the Masonic Building, big and unpartitioned as it was, made a refuge for many people, most of them older, though most of them were armed. The front door was stout, but it had two big street windows. These had woodwork bars nailed over them, sufficient screens against the wasps, but already badly splintered by the mantids.

Sheriff Smalls shouted, "Cluster-fire leftward! Those shutters are caving in!"

In the arc of the defenders' line, Smalls stood point—knelt point, with so many guns firing from either side. The Georges Junior and Senior flanked him—George Senior seated in a chair whose backrest helped him bear the recoil of his shotgun. Flanking them and a yard behind were two young Rasmussen men and two McCaufields—fourth generation natives of the same stripe. A second line of older defenders had at its center Iris Meyer, her right shoulder thickly padded, and the wheels of her chair locked to damp recoil.

Near eighty people sat or lay behind, their gazes fixed on the fanged heads and spiked arms thrusting ever farther through the spray of glass and splinters.

The right window's frame caved inward from the pressure. Two mantids erupted all the way inside, the uppermost launching off the lower's back. This forced the lower to falter in its assault, and it suffered swift amputation of its left grasper, but helped loft the upper bug, so that one landed and threatened the Georges with its graspers.

George Junior thrust himself in front of his father to shield him. His first shot was off, only tearing a chunk from the thorax, and, off-balance already, the recoil dropped him to his knees before the brute.

But in the instant the graspers hinged out for him, his father seized him from behind in both arms, thrusting his son's head down and his own forward.

Receiving the jaws himself, his head was engulfed, his neck sheared. His son, beneath them both, howled grief and rage, tilted up his barrel, and blew the killer's graspers off with their barbs still lodged in his father.

Heavy gunfire raged beyond the shutters. The bugs crowding the break in the frame began to be jolted, taken apart from the sides while their forelegs still struggled for entry.

"Holy shit!" shouted a young McCaufield happily. "The cavalry's coming! What a clusterfuck!"

"OK," barked Smalls. "Get closer now! Trim off their barbs from below!"

Flanking their splintering barriers they crouched—tough postures for the older defenders—and began to bring down a clattery rain of sundered graspers, while the focused fire outside still whittled the invaders away.

A new danger arose inside with this turning tide: lopped parts puddling to gel, and melon-sized blobs pouring forth in attack.

"Flame in here! Flame here!" bellowed Smalls. "George Junior, get that door ready to open!"

Still wiping tears from his eyes, George did so. When the first flame-team burst in, Smalls shouted, "Small gas-bursts! Just get a little flame on each of 'em!"

The team got good at this light-touch torching. Their foam-spray backup had to kill some blazes on the floorboards, but soon they had a dozen little globes quivering and vague in their movement, lit only on top, but already beginning to flatten.

# XXV
# FINGERS FALTER ON THE KEYBOARD

**Relentless artist that** he was, Val never stopped keying his visual music, adjusting, steering the flow of his forces, but he now faced a grave challenge.

The raft-gunners had been lethal. His own hands and those of his App control crew had toiled on their keyboards to reknit the programs that gunfire had scrambled in his cocoons. Many not blown to shreds had retained most of their tissue.

Now, an hour into the First Act, it was Lazarus-come-forth time. And bug after bug hatched inoperably deformed.

Graspers merged with midlegs, or wholly legless, or half-winged or half-headless. They hatched, plunged straight off their trees, and crashed dead.

Val had lost sixty-four mantids still in cocoon. A stunning blow.

He'd known these extras would be tough. He'd wanted a battle, of course. But today he'd gotten a broken nose in the first round. The dangerous coals of anger glowed in him. He must not be angry.

The APP death toll for Act One already was harrowing. Bad enough their emergence into a sleet of gunfire, but the extras' kill rate in the streets was accelerating. They developed tactics so quickly, shield-men to snag the graspers; paired swordsmen or shotgunners to sunder them.

His mantids, his lovely monsters! He'd been too enamored of their image, their glamorous monstrosity, to see their operational limitations.

Highly mobile and quick in their seizure—but narrowly frontal in their assault, and thus, in attack, poorly defended on both flanks. And building them with the bulk and leverage to snatch a man off his feet, he'd made them just a bit awkward against multiple assailants.

The upshot was, at the close of this act, he might withdraw well under two hundred APPs from the set. And assailed by so few, the extras would kill many more in Act Two.

Val had erred. His fingers had faltered on the keyboard of creation, and he was taking a grave beating. With APP-loss at this rate, his third act would be a farce, a festive town bug-hunt, conducted by the extras with jeers and hilarity!

But what of it? Was this too not a perfect story? The town triumphant! *Alien Death* itself all slain! It would be the first heartwarming Live Action ever shot! A giga-blockbuster!

But here Val hit a wall in himself. The town triumphant was not an option. He must not, would not go down so roundly beaten. His legions must not be swept from the field before the moon reached its zenith. Yet with all his forces fighting, what weapon did he have?

A notion stirred. "A dark moment," he murmured, a smile twitching his lips. "Dark as . . . a mineshaft."

Val woke a screen he'd not yet used on-shoot, for what it controlled had been entombed before the cameras rolled. He commed his lead raft of APP Control.

"You tracking their director's rafts, Aidan?"

"Roger that, Val. Both Devlin's and Harms' are working low, and we got rooftop assaults in place for them."

"Good. Now listen sharp, please, Aidan."

Val laid his wish out concisely.

The APP-tech was silent for a moment. "I can't promise a yes, boss."

Val smiled. "Life's a gamble. If we can get it out of there, it means a tour de force for the Third Act. I want full uplink and override of your operation, please—all your command patterns, gel sensorium, and enviro readouts up on my alpha screen. Think bright-side, Aidan: what if it works?"

He viewed his alpha screen, and he was instantly deep in

the earth. The lost APPs' sensorium—all his buried gel's tactile and visual experience of the colossal tomb that clasped it—was a weave of hair-thin fibers, mere molecules in thickness, probing for micro-pores in the crumbled planet-bone—for fissures up through the cave-in. There were, Val mused . . . eighty fingers at work on Properties' keyboards. It was like eighty fingers threading a million needles in a benthic darkness of crushing pressures.

So rapt he was in this that he almost missed—on one of the two screens devoted to his vid-thieves, Mark and Razz—a payoff from his preparations. It came in the act's last moments. In Devlin's raft, his APP crew had got a mantid aboard. Her reaction: instantaneous. But not quite quick enough—Val smiled when he saw—and not without a pleasant bit of vengeance.

**Half a minute** before Act One's end, Sandy Devlin had a rare careless moment. It was the joy of the kill that misled her, she hanging just two stories high with a southeast angle on the bug swarm at the Majestic's entry. From bow and stern she and Radner were gunning the shit out of mantids.

And then, from a rooftop behind them, a mantid leapt into their raft square amidships, and lunged for the pinioned Millar.

Sandy whipped the raft upside down, and the mantid's graspers had to cling for support, but its jaws just missed Mark's head, and sheared off instead his outhrust hand and forearm.

A barrel roll flung the bug free from the craft. The act ended seconds later, and she and Radner rushed to work on Mark's spouting stump. They got a pressure cup on it, and slammed his veins with anti-shock and tranks and Amelior—though amidships had gotten pretty slick and sticky by the time they were done. Sandy took a pad of gauze and began wiping Mark's blood off his displays.

Mark was gazing at the sky. Or more precisely, he'd raised his left arm's stump, and was gazing where his hand and forearm had been, but where now was only sky. Quietly, marveling, he said, "I'm . . . a character in this story."

Radner said, "Yeah. It's called, 'real life.' "

"That's . . . only part of what I meant. . . ."

Sandy said, "So this character's still a director, right? A renegade director stealing his master's shoot? For fame, and a shitload of clacks?"

Mark raised now his right hand against the sky, and flexed his five remaining digits. "Yes . . ." he mused. "I believe he is."

He began keying, sifting the first act's footage, his lone hand tentative at first without its mate, then taking firmer hold, rummaging more greedily through its harvest.

Sandy commed Smalls. "So where's that sonofabitch Razz?"

"He kept ducking us in the fight. I think he's into it. Real good with that shotgun. Not in sight now, gone inside somewhere."

"Well keep bullhorning him! Appeal to his professional pride. He's a goddam director an' we'll let him direct!"

. . .

**Val wouldn't violate** his contract with this town, wouldn't assault them in the entr'acte. He'd put that temptation behind him.

But he had no contract with Razz. Interlopers broke the rules, and couldn't claim the rules' protection. No need to kill him. Mark Millar's mishap—his almost slapstick amputation—offered a useful alternative to homicide.

**Since he was** young, Razz had always regretted he'd never been to war.

Combat! It was . . . transcendence! Ecstasy was standing outside yourself. The fight had been like an ugly, deafening ecstasy! What a rush!

He now comprehended why they had put guns in his hands the instant he'd showed up—why they'd trusted him: once it started, they were all one body. He'd saved two people's lives within the first ten minutes, and three others had saved his.

He'd never known you could feel this together with other people, strangers who were no longer strangers once the shit hit the fan. Never had he felt so completely alive. His spine was like a fine-tuned violin, and the prickly bowstring of danger kept stroking it with adrenaline.

Now, in the entr'acte, he was still fighting for his side, but keeping discreetly out of sight in case they tried to stick him back aboard his raft. He was on a search-and-destroy patrol, yeah! Looking for laired gel on pause-mode, to rout it out and torch it. Make the fight safer for his fellow soldiers.

He'd searched one building, then peered carefully out into the street, and darted over and into the structure beside it, a three-story Victorian.

On the street floor, Fran's Boutique. A smell of new clothes and cosmetics. Bouquets in a glass-doored refrigerator. Down behind the counter . . . ? Clear.

Up the stairway to the next floor, at its turning, was a closet. Nothing in it but coats, brooms, a vacuum.

The floor above was an apartment—Fran's, he guessed. The living room looked out on the street. There was a closet here too, and this one's door was slightly ajar.

He opened it, and bingo.

Déjà vu. This sphere of gel was as big as the one under that building—a huge greenish-black pearl, at rest in the shadow. Recalling his abject terror that first time, he smiled. So much better to be on the offensive, be a fighter.

It couldn't be burned here. It could be rolled, he knew—hard, sluggish work, but it ought to go down the stairs quick enough, with gravity helping. He didn't much like to touch it with his bare hands, though. He took a light jacket from its hanger. He made a two-handed glove of it, a hand halfway down each sleeve, leaned over the globe . . . and paused.

Faintly sketching its interior, there were furtive smudges of pale luminescence. What had it consumed, to reach this mass? Surely half a man, or big parts of several men.

Perhaps it was this thought that gave him an impulse to see the globe as a big, dark eyeball, and the blurred greenish glints in its depths like fleeting, malignant thoughts.

It was of course a kind of eye, a camera.

Razz had the sudden sensation of looking straight into Val Margolian's eyes. He tingled with the feeling, his brain struggling to tear it down. Would Val himself actually be bothering to screen all his dormant gel's sensoria?

And Razz, in his spine, knew that question's answer. For Val Margolian was Razz's Dark God, was colossal Chronos to Razz's young Zeus. Val was the best. And yes, he would be screening everything.

Young Zeus, far more tensely poised now, conceded to himself that he was beginning to shit some bricks here.

Just stop now. He was being paranoid.

The sphere collapsed—a suddenness that seemed impossible in such dense mass—and though he leapt back spring-quick, it engulfed his left foot to the shin.

He launched himself toward the stairs. Pulled short mid-leap, he slammed to the floor facedown, and scrambled like a lizard on all fours—all threes, his snagged foot dragging sluggishly behind and freezing cold now.

Excruciating cold and brutal pressure on that foot, a crushing freeze that climbed his calf and shin, had him almost to the knee now as his hands reached the rim of the first step. Like a Hercules he hauled himself toward it, just as what clenched him broke free of its anchoring mass, and he slithered bumping on his belly down the first flight of stairs.

Freed of the dreadful weight that had detained him, but with all his lower leg now in its vise of ice, he scrambled down the last flight in its turn, clawed himself upright against the wall, and began hopping for the front door. Tripped on the doorsill, pitched out across the porch, and rode down the porch steps too on his face, shouting, shouting.

Help converged, and only then, as he felt hands lifting him by the shoulders, did he look at his leg.

A marrow-freezing sight. The gel, swelling like a monstrous tick, was some ten inches in diameter and in length! Beyond that tarry knot beneath his knee, was nothing else!

Even as they shot the meds and dope in him, he watched the gel grow spherical, consuming the last inch of him it gripped, and falling free. And then it rested there on the street, unmoving—as if to say, "I'm done! Come get me"—till it was swiftly gassed and burned.

"Just kind of a little spanking from Val, don't you think?"

It was Sandy from her raft just above him. He looked up at her from the haze of the pain-meds and the anti-shock. "I mean," Sandy elaborated, smiling, "that was a personal little transaction between you and him. He just gave us that gel to be torched—like a tip. I guess he wants you in your raft like we all do! He wants all your following shots down here. And what that suggests to me, Razz, is that Val expects to own *your* footage as well as his own!"

# XXVII
# THE LAST ENTR'ACTE

**The sun was** perhaps seven diameters above the western horizon. Moonrise would be a few minutes past sunset, then twelve or thirteen minutes later the silver disc would come all the way up, and take the whole town into the gaze of its great eye.

Just under a hundred-thirty APPs had been salvaged from the slaughter that had ended with the sun's declining. The extras had well over three hundred effectives still in the field.

What the moon would soon beam down on here, would

be an out-and-out bug-hunt from the moment that Act III opened.

Like a fighter who's had an arm amputated just before the final round—that was the feeling Val had to wrestle down in his heart. He wanted to smite his foes in the field with whole batallions, and what he had were battered remnants, some missing legs, parts of wings, chunks of heads.

As for reinforcements? These were still locked in the earth. These were black filaments a quarter mile long, worming and weaving through hundreds of meters of dense mountain rubble.

But they were rising faster now, and faster still with each passing minute. All his rafts were pouring their spare signal strength into his Properties computers. The filaments toiled upward like worms in a feeding frenzy. He might yet enter Armageddon armed. He keyboarded like Poppa Bach.

Again he wondered, at this *cheating*? To override so diligently the natural outcome of his shoot? He'd brought his great Mayhem Machine here, it had been met in battle by the spirit of these fierce defenders, and look at the heart warming end that his tale was tending to: the extras victorious. Screw it all! I'm the artist and my say goes!

For behold, in twenty years, how many monsters he had created—all designed to work his will. Each one himself. He was a spielmeister. A master of the game. And for the first time in his career, it was a game he'd made his players play. Val knew himself at last. Of course he was a monster.

He smiled. A peace, a tranquil power filled him. This was . . . completeness. He had at last evicted from his heart a sullen stowaway, a ceaselessly muttering enemy in his own mind, insisting he was something he was not: a critic of his culture, confronting it with its own brutal obsessions; schooling it.

What horseshit! What a cozy crock! He was a punisher. He was a scourge.

He was in fact—after all these years—still a teacher. But a teacher of the truer sort, one who taught in the medium of flesh and blood—like all great leaders, all great generals. His will and his art were one at last, a seamless whole. He filled himself completely for the first time.

Look now at his opponents. Ah, they were diligent and sly—a lot of them lined up at the hardware store, being issued . . . galoshes! Even taking the three pairs of them off the manikins in the window.

He thought a moment, and then got it. Their keenness, their resourcefulness. Truly these people were artists themselves. How much they gave to his story. What a partnership he had created here.

And their diligence honed his advantage. Having borne out their newly dead, their focus was in town now, reinforcing refuges, resupplying armaments. Val began to wake the dormant gel that hid everywhere in alleys and under foundations. Sneaking it in subtle filaments along the angles where walls met earth or pavement, delicately stitching it through every part of town toward his point of collection.

And never ceasing as he did so to blend his keyboarding then with that of his APP-meisters, amplifying their signals with his own, sucking his buried giant up through the rubble of the mine shaft and flexing it as it rose to widen each little aperture, so that what came following poured more amply upward.

**In the first** minutes of the entr'acte, in the slanted sun of the waning day, lovers and friends found each other and embraced, rejoicing, each to the other a treasure still possessed, despite all the death that had just stormed among them.

"You know what you are?" Gillian said to Chops—said to his chest, where her face was snuggled. "You're a little wolf."

"Who're you callin *little*?"

"*Big* I said," she giggled. "A *big* wolf."

"Then you"—he stroked her thick black Native-American hair—"are a little mink."

"You calling me a minx?"

"What's a *minx*?"

Kate Harlow gripped Japh's shoulders and pushed him off to arm's length. Fixing his eyes sternly with hers. "Brace yourself, big guy. I'm moving in."

"You're already moved in."

"I mean full-time."

**Back in the** church's little rectory, Momma Grace got a nice urn of coffee brewed for the women under her care, and while they were filling their cups, she brewed herself a cup of tea.

She took this back to the preacher's dais, and sat down

near the pulpit, where Auntie Drew's body lay wrapped in its blanket. She absently wiped the tears from her eyes, took another sip of her tea, and then spoke quietly to her precious friend.

"You know dear . . . about this talk of attacking the studio that's going around. Lord knows I understand. They are all amped from battle, but so many of our sweet friends have died already, and even more would die if we did that. What do you think of it, Drew?"

Again she sipped tea, thoughtfully. And answered for her friend. "Well, Gracie, I suppose I have mixed feelings. Precious friends, yes—we've lost so many! But I can't help thinking what all of them would want from us now. I think they would want us—forgive me, dear—to kill every one of those sons of bitches we could."

Momma Grace wiped her eyes again, and smiled. "Thank you, dear. I feel the same. I suppose I just didn't want to be the first to say it."

Our new dead numbered forty-one, and as many again were badly hurt. But grim though this was, we took heart, because the tide had dramatically turned. They'd been slaughtering the mantids by shoot's end.

I wrapped a hug around Jool. Her little belly snuggled against me, but the fight was still in her arms and shoulders, and it took holding her a while before she could relax against me.

We went out into the street. Some folks were reinforcing refuges, others tending the wounded. I had tears in my eyes. Even after death our friend helped us. Without his swords and shields we could never have turned the battle. I remembered first seeing him, in that packed car in the 'tube. His eight-ball head and the glint of that gold tooth, the two of us on our way to be extras in *Alien Hunger,* and dance with the giant spiders.

We sat on the library porch, leaned back against the wall, half-dozing together. Snugglers like us were everywhere on the street. There was a quiet rejoicing in the air. The part of us that had just carried dead friends from where they had fallen hadn't stopped grieving, but, come moonrise, we saw only our revenge ahead of us, and no more of us dying.

Someone was gently kicking the sole of my foot. We'd passed out. The sun was near setting, and here was Chops, with Gillian at his side. People were busy everywhere, checking arms, yelling in position. Chops squatted, leaning close to talk low. "We've been passing this around. It's just a thought been bothering us. . . ."

Gillian too got close. "We were fighting the street last act," she told us. "Some stray fire took a chunk off the top of the bank behind us, big piece of concrete that slammed down on a gel-blob rolling toward us. Smashed it flat center-mass. The two end segments globed up and rolled away either side. Then the chunk, like, moved, and a little sheet of gel edged out from under it, thinner than paper, and it globed up and rolled away."

She hesitated. Chops said gently, "Just tell 'em, Gillian."

"Sometimes I . . . feel things in the ground. A couple times in Oregon when I was a kid. There was a little earthquake once, and I felt it coming—maybe ten minutes before it happened."

"Like an aura," I said.

"I guess so. And a couple years later, when it had been raining for weeks, I felt something coming from the next hill over, and I hiked over that way, and just as I got in sight of it there was a landslide, a sizeable one that took some trees down with it.

"So I'm saying I felt something up at the mine, guys. Right after the last act ended. I took an ATV up there and I swear I felt movement in it. Nothing you could see or hear, but I felt it."

"Sounds to me," Jool said, "like somebody should go up and check it out again."

And I had to agree. "He'd never have meant for us to exterminate his bugs, and that's what he's looking at right now. Somebody better go up to the shaft and check it out."

"Smalls is taking some three-wheelers up in a few minutes," Gillian said. "Wants you along, Curtis."

**The greatest vid** director who had ever lived. Val knew himself serenely, absently, the same way his fingertips danced on his keys, and his eyes worked his screens: enraptured, unhurried.

The enemy was strong and cunning. There, even now, was a squad of their tripods roaring up toward the mine—just a half mile away from it and closing . . . and just at this moment, he brought the last thread of his buried gel out of the rubbly spoil that choked the shaft.

He rivered it down into the grass, to join the braid of other threads, to pour them in one smooth, slender cable that already stretched more than a mile toward Sunrise.

His fingers deftly hastened it, but his serpent, it seemed,

was a tad sluggish, a bit awkward in response. Its rivering had a ripply rhythm to it, a slight liquid lurch as it flowed, causing the grass to tremor, faintly betraying its passage even in the moon's deceptive light. Explosive burial had damaged its synapses somewhat. . . . But not too much, no. It could do what he intended.

A half mile farther, and here the futile search party came, clustering round the shaft mouth. Let them grope and scratch their heads like chimps. A quarter mile farther down now he'd brought its questing tip . . . and yet a farther quarter mile . . . and now he had it snaking down into the industrial zone. . . .

Just then—spot on time—he saw the moon had cleared the peaks. He commed Properties. "Aidan. Deploy the APPs as we discussed, and wait for my order."

Up the rear walls of buildings they brought the mantids, brought them low across rooftops, scuttling them out along walls in the shadows of alleys. All of them simply deploying, none striking, none showing themselves.

An interlude of pure hiatus. Moon up, the whole town clenched in readiness . . . and nothing happened. It made marvelous in-the-street footage: everyone watchful, the arms trucks and fire trucks cycling up and down the blocks . . . and nothing happening. Everywhere you felt the enemy they scanned for but did not find.

Steadily Val poured the serpent of his reinforcements to their collection point. The gel of his avenger was no longer what it had been—his directive signals had to be multiplied to impel it accurately. The stresses of its burial had taken a toll. His last-act titan might prove slightly retarded . . . but it would serve.

His art was Death—so what? Most die randomly, alone, without a context or grand struggle. Those who died here Val lifted with himself—their saga's Maker—out of Death, dark and entire, into an afterlife that would blaze and battle as long as humankind sucked vid.

Time to open the ball, get the surviving bugs moving. "Aidan? Action!"

And round every corner, from the rooftops, his APPs flowed down onto the façades of the buildings and began swarming across them in all directions. The guns woke up everywhere, trying to track their crazy currents along the walls. Drawn fire blew a floodlight out and half a block went dark. One mantid dove from the wall, plunging jaws-first, and sheared an extra's head off down to the collarbone.

"That's good," he told Aidan. "Scatter your kills the whole length of town. Sustain till my next com."

He kept keying. Just a quarter mile of gel left to thread into his secret weapon.

**"How many klicks** can this hit in three seconds, max acceleration?" A calmly posed question—by Sandy Devlin to duct-taped Mark Millar.

"Three-fifty." Mark was terse—still dazed, but in a remote way that left his five remaining fingers limber, agile on the keyboard. These visuals! Though this had cost him half an arm, look what he was getting here!

But suddenly the words he'd just uttered—"three-fifty"—seized him bodily, crushed him down into his seat with the forces of acceleration. Sandy swooped in a swift maneuver—had snatched with their raft's tow hook a mantid straight out of the air by its neck. And now accelerating skyward at a rate he thought might crush him, he saw the flailing bug hauled helplessly through the air astern of them.

They streaked down toward the trees below town, hooked a skyward arc at crushing acceleration—climbing, climbing as they arced back up over the shoot. Mark struggled to read what Devlin was doing, but was still a half beat behind when she did it—hit the hook release as she dove down over a sizeable shoot-raft, and sent the mantid, wide-winged and struggling in the air, straight down amidships of what Mark instantly knew—seeing Aidan Zadok there at the helm—was the chief APP-control raft of Margolian's Properties squadron.

# XXVII
## AND THE DEAD SHALL BE RAISED

**The spasmodic din** of gunfire could be heard all along the street, especially the dark blocks. The dizzying dance of the bugs, little squads of them darting multidirectionally across the building fronts, had tricked their machine-gun fire into destroying three floodlights, dark and lit blocks alternating now. In the pauses of gunfire the fighters' shouts filled the air, the bugs' erratic flow waking everywhere outcries and warnings, pulling the troops' eyes in all directions.

It was a kind of bug guerilla warfare, Japh thought. He'd left his thirty-cal, grabbed a third twelve-gauge, and gone mobile, watching walls as he jogged for shifts in the bug-flow that he could run to meet, blowing off their legs as they came.

He heard above the boil of voices, "On your left!"—An odd note to the voice, odd too its high angle of origin. He looked left, saw nothing, looked right and saw a man facing him from five yards away, gun at ready, and saw a bug drop off the wall behind him and bite his head clean off.

He was already shotgunning it before the headless man's knees had buckled and dumped him.

Lots of other firing now, bugs triggering a new lead-storm seemingly everywhere. He saw heavy bug-assault on the next block and ran to it, adding his twelve's fire-tongues to the defense against the rippling squads of bugs that shifted formation and flowed back up the walls.

But they'd got enough legs off of one to drop it to the street, shield-snagged its graspers and chopped them right off—all while Japh was feeling some uncompleted thought hanging fire in his brain. Then, watching them torch the big gel-pool they'd made, it came to him.

The guy who'd lost his head, facing Japh, was turned to his left, and the voice had come down from above him. And the Sunrisers themselves had mostly deserted the rooftops because bringing the APPs down to the street was the surest way to kill them.

And the voice itself was odd. "On your left." But really it was more like "Ong urr lefk!" He thought he heard his name shouted. Then heard it clearer.

"Japh! Someone's trapped in here—gotta be bugs in there!"

It was Chops, standing in front of Cap's Hardware, and as Japh ran toward him, called, "Get my back!" and went into the store.

And just as Japh got there, he heard from the dark interior what Chops must have heard: "In here!"

Except that it was slightly more like "Ing-geeere!"

Chops was standing inside in the dark saying, "Where . . . ?"—and Japh rushed in after him saying, "Shhh!"

But Chops got it already, stood poised with his twelve up, scanning the shadows, softly saying, "Where's the light switch?"

"By the counter I think."

As if the dark in here dimmed sound as well as light, the uproar in the street seemed half a world away. The window sent a dim slab of moonlight a few yards inside, spiked by the three shadows of the manikins, and Chops stood poised just at the edge of it.

"They have *voices*," Japh murmured, and Chops nodded. Japh came farther in to stand at his flank, struggling to think. The big double back door that opened on the loading dock showed panes of even dimmer light because the dock was canopied, but it looked firmly shut. But wasn't there another way in here? What was it?

This was a big space in front of them, two long stock shelves splitting its floor in three lanes, the main counter and a smaller counter beyond them, the tat-chair's nook—all full of shadow. Chops muttered, "It'll dry-gulch us in there, we gotta *draw* it."

In the pane of dim light they shared, one of the manikins' shadows fell between them.

"Wait," Japh hissed. He darted back to the window. After an instant's hesitation, laid by his twelve and grabbed up one of the dummies by the waist. Unwieldy with all the tools she wore, she was some work to waltz back toward Chops.

"You stand my flank and we'll fish with her."

He crouched low behind and edged her into the darkness of the center aisle, advancing very slowly but turning her left and right to amplify her movement.

And just as he'd started this ruse, the answer that had eluded him leapt back to memory . . . the basement door was in that wall fifteen feet to his right and those basements communicated now, and there must be bugs inside many of the buildings.

Almost knocking Chops over, he jumped back from the aisle and hoisted the dummy high to his right toward a sudden chitinous bug noise, and felt a barb tear through the web of his thumb as tool-girl's head, helmet and all, was engulfed by a bug, its graspers hauling her up out of his hands.

And then it was fighting to free its arms, the dummy's tough plastic tightly trapping its barbs.

"Legs!" Chops shouted, pulling his second gun. When they'd blown both legs off one side it toppled. It lifted its other pair, scrabbling at the air, making them harder to blow off. And in the brief silences between shots as they whittled them away, they heard a swift scuttle of claws across the roof above their heads.

"Oh shit! Get its arms!" Japh shouted, and ran back to the window just as a mantid erupted through the front door. He had to drop his second gun to seize the second manikin in time. Heaved it up and swung it around in such lucky synchronicity with the bug's assault that he tucked her shoulders in its barbs and her head in its mouth in one smooth thrust.

He glanced to see Chops just taking off his bug's remaining arm. Grimly Japh unholstered his third gun. As the mantid fought to free its barbs from its prey, Japh set to work methodically, first, blowing off its head . . .

**Aidan, the Properties** chief, was a desperately busy man. Val had just commed him to "Send half the troops in—eat 'em up. When that half's down, send in the other half!"

There was an oddly merry tone to that command—the boss had something big of his own going, apparently. But what a kill-fest his troops had jumped into. Those swords and shields began eating them up down there. He was afraid he would smile, and that Val's monitors would catch it.

Aidan, a wiry, redheaded, and very motivated kid from the Zoo, had worked himself all the way up from mean streets to this, his present lofty post, and while his fingers danced to kill them, his heart couldn't help exulting in the ass-kicking that Zoo-meat down there was giving his monsters.

Aidan had installed a little shunt in his cams to steal

footage from his shoots. When he drank with old Zoo friends up in his crib in the Hollywood Hills, they all viewed them laughing and shouting. Thus he shared his high life with pals who might themselves sign on as extras someday. Only a man born in the Zoo himself could understand how this was OK with his friends, how they could find in it a celebration of themselves.

Dutifully and skillfully his fingers toiled to keep his bugs alive, while thinking the whole awful game was beautiful. In the darker blocks where the battle had destroyed the floodlights, the gunfire was all flame-flashes in the moonlight, orange tongues of annihilation licking the air. And in the lit blocks, indelible cameos: a sinewy arm working the slide of a pump-gun, a fire team of two small, quick women, drenching and lighting a spill of gel in the instant it had contracted into a globe, a man toppling backward, his feet locked in a quick tongue of gel, then wrenching his feet from his rubber boots and scrambling backward on his ass as another fire team flanked in on him and drove the gel back in flames. . . .

Something slammed aboard Aidan's raft. He took one glance behind him, and threw the raft into a steep, fast dive, his sole aim to topple backward the mantid reaching for him.

He felt something like the collision of a Mack truck with his neck, and he was engulfed in darkness absolute. He was . . . only his *head*! He was dissolving! *Shit*. . . .

**Mark caught it** all. Aidan, though he dove his raft to throw the bug backward, was the first casualty, the monster then wheeling to snatch the life of one of his lieutenants, just before the raft crashed into a building.

And Mark saw, in the same instant, Razz's raft—himself at the cameras now, and that raft-jockey, Sharon Harms, at the controls—deliver a second bug to the raft of Slake Fincher, Aidan's co-chief of Properties. Slake thrust up an arm to save his head, and lost that arm to the shoulder, and in his convulsion yanked his raft into a backward tumble that flung—at the first flip—his crew and the APP into empty air, and went on tumbling to crash upside down on a rooftop.

Whoa! It would all be on Val now to manage his monsters, his *dwindling* monsters, which the extras were killing wherever Mark looked.

**Val was in** it now. Home, right in the eye of the hurricane he'd conjured. From here on out, his fleet must handle all else. His whole thought was down in his storm's vortex, keying his gel from half a dozen boards at once, letting the rest of his APPs go full-bore to attack. The crew must do as well as they could to keep them alive.

Henceforth his sole darling was the resurgent gel. The threads of it he had sneaked from all over the set, the great snake brought down from the mine—more than half of it had been sneaked into its final destination: the heaped dead of Sunrise in their hundreds.

In moonlight shadow his threads snaked unseen, crooking along the bases of buildings, crossing the old pavement along its cracks—all angling and crooking toward, all tucking in like tongues beneath that funeral pile of moon-pale faces.

Val's keying was exquisite, the gel absorbing what it rose beneath, condensing flesh and bone into its own supple density. The bier rose, but so incrementally! All those pale, moon-aimed faces, their slight shifts and liftings made them seem to dream. The augmentation of their mass would be inevitable soon, but with delicate chiselings from beneath he kept their topmost layer intact, a long human mask just rippling faintly, rising here and there, an anthropoid lid on a bulge of death a block long.

Almost there . . . Down the slopes came ATVs and three-wheelers. The locals were wise to Val, but not quite in time. He gave his screens an apologetic smile. Time to take the wraps off, and go big.

**We kept angling** our flash-beams this way and that on the rubble that choked the shaft mouth, but it didn't change things. There were half a dozen little rat holes in the rubble, the biggest two inches across, but dust-free, and showing narrow, smooth tracks through the loose earth below them. How many APPs had been down there? How much gel had he brought up?

"East side of town," said Smalls, his binocs scanning Sunrise below us. "There's no one fighting there—everyone's in the street fighting bugs."

I said, "He's going for our dead."

I didn't know my thought until I spoke it. It froze us all a moment, as we took it in. If the gel could incorporate our dead, it would grow gigantic. We fired up the three-wheelers, and went straight down the slopes, no time for the road's lazy curves.

It was like riding a flung stone skipping out across incoming waves—we were in the air more than half the time, hanging on desperately, our teeth gritted to keep them from rattling loose.

Halfway down we could make out that the heap of our dead looked larger. Smalls had commed, and we could see fighters running out into the Industrial Zone. We came down the last slope, and now could see—down where our dead had been—a bulge of darkness rising. The moonlight showed its surface clear, a long field of arms and faces aimed at the sky. All of them thinning and shrinking and melting away into the moon-shine. That big dome's mass half-filled the lot.

Then it englobed. The sight made the hair on my arms stand up. It was poised like a bubble now, the whole thing drenched in moonlight. And the moonlight showed its meal was not quite done. Within its mass were human fragments, limbs and heads almost transparent, faces thin as smoke.

Like a giant nullifier. What sick brain could think this up, let alone make it?

The huge sphere had some wobbliness to it—not the smooth tension we'd seen in small masses—but it tensed into a slightly tighter sphere, as if in some last effort of digestion . . . and then, it divided—thinned at the center forming two separate spheres, a shrinking bar joining them like a dumbbell, then tapering and parting. . . .

We roared onto the flats, gunning between and around

the globes, each bigger than a three-story house—and gunned flat-out for the alleys that would bring us—and them—out into the street.

"Lemme off here!" I yelled when we reached it. I had to get Jool, get her out of the church. She couldn't be trapped inside with this shit pouring in on her.

Everyone was shouting to everyone else but yet everyone hearing somehow. Our people crowded to the side of the street away from the eastern alley mouths where the gel would pour through. Meanwhile . . . something was happening to the mantids.

Those trying to kill people suddenly slowed down, moved more jerkily, while those not yet engaged paused and seemed vague in their movements.

And everywhere those on the walls were leaping down and moving slow and aimless among us.

"Cut 'em down quick!" someone blared from a megaphone and then I saw her. It was Ming—her face like a gorgon's ever since Mazy's death. She stood in a raft with a crumpled prow, hovering at rooftop level. Stood behind the raft's sole surviving pilot, a guy with blood on his face and Ming's shotgun snug to the back of his neck. He was keying his console frantically.

We closed in on the Mantids in a shit-storm of swords and twelves, lopped off not just their graspers, but their heads and their wings. Their lopped-off pieces were jouncing everywhere on the pavement and going to gel, and everywhere this gel was being gassed and torched, so that we fought like fire dancers high-stepping in flames as we hacked them in a fever of rage.

It was a festival under the Summer moon, the bugs like some strange crop that had grown from our pavements, and we the harvesters who reaped them with a vengeance.

I had to shake it off, this kill-fever, like a trance. Few bugs still stood and their gel was everywhere, and I remembered that a shitload more gel was coming through those alleys any moment. And as quick as we fired the gel around us, far more than half of it was escaping under buildings and snaking its way back to the giants in the Zone.

I had a thought, but saw Smalls was ahead of me—already had fire teams up on the rooftops flanking the alleys.

And then it dawned on me: a new danger threatened us all.

I needed a second pair of hands! I looked around, and saw Ricky Dawes.

"Hey Ricky! You gotta come help me! Quick!"

And as we ran past an alley mouth, there came a tsunami of gel, filling it like a piston.

We sprinted down Glacier. "They'll think of the hydrants soon enough," I shouted to Ricky as we ran, "but we'll need more water than that."

We hooked out of town at the south end and ran toward the water tower, veered just before it, and sprinted up into the City Yard. And all the way there I was thinking of Val Margolian and hating that crafty, cold-hearted son of a bitch with all my soul. The fucker was planning to make us help him burn Sunrise to the ground.

. . .

**Val tested his** giants on the defenders who rushed back into the Yard to meet them. He recoiled them from the gas-sprays, and in the next instant counter-surged toward them in thick tongues that seized half a dozen people waist high, and dragged them under.

But though quick in action his spheres were balky and wobbly. He should have caught a score of people on that rush—could now only pour his gel in pursuit just fast enough that their retreat marred their counter-fire. Both his globes caught some flame, which he swallowed up in their rolling flow.

There was another wobbly lurch and seizure of an extra who stumbled, but again the gel took new fire. This again he engulfed . . . yet saw now within the gel's bulk a flash of angry orange cancer, the blaze encysted, and only half-smothered.

The last mantid . . . gone. No forces here left to him with which to distract the extras' defense. He saw too the rooftop fire teams flanking the alleys he must enter, and knew he could not emerge from those gauntlets unscathed.

And saw then, all at once, that entirely new tactics were at his disposal here. This situation could be shaped to an unforgettable end, to the archetypic climax of combat: a bright apocalypse consuming everything.

They wanted to torch him, did they? No. He was the torch! He'd let them ignite him, and then he would take their whole damned town.

His last scene glowed full-blown before his mind's eye. Stunning! The orange light of flames devouring the moonlight. A huge, flourishing garden of flame in the shape of a town! Steeples and cornices, porches and doorways and window frames blooming and blazing and bannering crimson and gold! All of us felt it, didn't we? That surge of Bacchanal, of festival in a total firestorm.

What a lovely conspiracy he and Sunrise had going between them. They did not foresee the crimson canvas they were going to help him paint. They would kindle his palette, and he would paint the town with it.

So. Now to send his giants through the alleys. Not too fast, neither too slow . . .

He morphed the globes into a pair of obese worms, tapered slugs twenty-feet thick and seventy long. He poured them into the alleys, his fingers hyper-dexterous, incessantly correcting and overriding that quiveriness and that lurking sloth in his earth-wounded monsters.

Gas rained on them, and flares came hissing down after. Both giants sprouted a dorsal crest of flames. Faster now, faster! Both torches were lit, and their blaze must be shared, before they lost the mass and the strength to distribute it.

Now came truly transcendental keyboarding, a music he must not mar with thought or hesitation. His artistry at this juncture was trancelike. Or disjuncture rather, for he split both worms lengthwise as he brought them out into the street, and diverged their halves down the sidewalks. And he set these half-worms to smearing their mass along the building fronts, smearing great stripes of flaming gel across porches and walls and doorways.

The ignited gel clung to those surfaces, long scabs of fire

that bit into its new fuel. Four whole blocks . . . now six blocks striped with fierce-biting fire.

Then he rolled the mega-worms—smoking, but their fire mostly shed—laterally out across the street to meet new gas-and-torch assaults from the troops ranked to front them.

Still his weapons had mass enough to bear the new blazes the extras crowned them with—to keep steamrolling forward, forcing the defenders to stream laterally down the sidewalks, pour round their ends, and to start spraying and flaming their street-ward flanks.

But from that deployment, the defenders were helpless to stop Val's giants from painting the other side of those blocks with fire as well.

And—suddenly, it seemed—they were not such giants anymore. At last, their titan strength was broken. They had ceased answering his keystrokes. They tremored now, slumping away from the walls they'd torched, feebly twisted and thrashed, and lay inert, shriveling as the flames died down.

An odd sense of ceremony filled him. Val rested his hands on his lap. *Satis est.* His piece was played, its coda echoing. Long scars, swift-growing scars of fire lit the shadows of the moon-drenched street, snapping and snarling as they gnawed the night with their yellow fangs.

A gem. A faceted jewel of split-second improvisation. He was getting older, true enough, but had lost not a jot of his gift for riding the moment, for snatching inspiration from the heat of battle. See the blaze roar in its feasting!

. . .

**I knew that** Sunrise had a pair of small water trucks with two thousand-gallon tanks—for out-of-town homesteads with poor wells that stored the water in tanks of their own. Each truck carried forty feet of three-inch canvas hose for off-loading. The trucks had off-load pumps too in them, that could put out a powerful stream.

In the Yard we were just upslope enough to see, under the smoke pouring up, licks of flame rising up into sight here and there.

We filled the truck's tank from a secondary tank in the yard fed by the water tower. It was agony, waiting to take on that load. At last I drove out with it, leaving Ricky to fill the second truck.

My vehicle was unwieldy, wallowing dreadfully on the downslope curves of the maintenance road.

Wrestling it down to the south end of town now, swinging onto Glacier . . .

Great, snarling stripes of fire, both sides of the street. Blocks of fire! Huge cinders of burnt gel littered the pavement.

"Help here!" I shouted. "Man my pump!"

The street had two hydrants. People were already clustered at both of them, and others were hurrying from the Majestic, carrying the hoses kept stored there. The gel had acted as an accelerant, was all but shriveled already, but had gotten the wood fiercely started.

I took up the hose, climbed on top of the tank, and got one guy to drive me up onto the sidewalk and close to the nearest wall. Then got another to start up the pump. We drove the truck down along the sidewalk, drenching flames and sending black smoke and white geysering up at the moon.

There was Ricky now, pulling up into the street's far end. The squads got their hoses hooked up, and water was snarling and hissing as it bit into fire. Everywhere people formed relays for buckets of water from the houses. Steam and smoke were everywhere, our shouts drowning out the roar of flames.

Until at last came the moment when we saw that all along the street the fire was lessening. Saw it raged only here and there, its smoke climbing in thicker and thicker columns.

And then we knew. We had won. That hissing noise of drenched flames sounded like a sigh, a huge sigh of relief that the whole town was breathing. The assault on Sunrise had been repelled. Sunrise had survived.

It struck me then—and not me alone—that all of our dead friends and loved ones had fought with us and helped us to the very end. They had all entered the monster's flesh and weakened it. They had turned it to fuel for our flames. All our dear dead had risen again to fight at our sides.

We had conquered at great cost. Some building-fronts' siding had been half-consumed, the charred, naked studs showing through. Shingle roofs had been more than half consumed, their charred joists like the bones of carnage. But Sunrise was still standing.

I went up to one of the big gel cinders and stood looking at it. I wasn't the only one doing this, dreamlike, standing in the steamy, puddled street, thinking of all the lost friends entombed in there. Glittery-wet with our firefighting streams, they were studded and spiked with the shapes they'd contained, or engulfed. Half-melted heads with charred eyeglobes joined to human skulls, shrunken arms and legs protruding, a foot, sole skyward as if the rest of its owner had dived into oblivion. One profiled face, its eye a moon-aimed onyx, cupped water like its dying tears.

We looked at one another. Down the whole length of Glacier, people stood talking in pairs and trios, or just stood holding each other, the taller heads tenderly laid on the lower—not as if after a battle, but with the air of drowsy lovers ready for rest, sharing quiet thoughts. Our words rose in a murmur, as if the silence of all our dead had muted us as well.

Then heads began turning toward the boulevard's midpoint. A faint disk of light had appeared on the pavement, a light more golden than the moon's, and growing stronger. A shaft of this light was beaming down from above.

A raft up there was beaming it. The street went mute. From the raft a bulky shadow sank toward us on a cable that, released in the spotlight, proved to be a bale of something in shiny shrink-wrap.

The cable was retracted as the raft slid to the west side of the street and tilted its bow slightly downward to show us Val Margolian, seated behind his console. He smiled. One side of his head was bandaged. His voice came at a mellow amplification that reached the whole street.

"Your payout is three hundred million, three hundred thousand, three hundred dollars. We've rounded it up a bit, just for the symmetry of the number.

"We now most sincerely salute you all for the heroic defense you've waged. We are pleased to tell you that Panoply has brokered your full pardon from the State, though the ratio of capital punishments you've actually suffered tallies far below the mandate of your sentence."

I only realized how amazing it was when it had continued for several heartbeats: our perfect universal silence, every one of us standing there mute, looking up at him.

This silence seemed to tell him something that he had not expected, something that made his pleasant expression become a shade more thoughtful.

"It's with the deepest respect that I tell you you've been the most courageous opponents we have ever faced. Opponents, we were of cruel necessity. We could not change the fate that had befallen you, but together, you and Panoply have fashioned something from that fate that will never be forgotten.

"Not one of your deaths will end the life it took. All those lives' endings will be woven into a tapestry that will be studied, that will be relived by whole generations to come."

Margolian had begun this statement gravely, earnestly, but the unbroken silence below him, all our eyes coldly studying him, changed his tone as he spoke till it grew almost strident by the time he finished.

Sheriff Smalls and some helpers had approached the bale and razored off its wrappings, and—still in silence—stood counting packets of bills for some moments. Margolian sat up there watching us all, as if we were a vid that was turning out stranger than he had expected.

At length, Smalls straightened up, and spoke the only answer Sunrise had for him that night:

"The amount seems in order. We'll make use of this."

# FORTRESS HOLLYWOOD

**Later that year,** just after our second snowstorm, I was watching Jool nursing Lyla. This was delightful to me—I couldn't stop grinning—to watch our avid little pap-sucker, her tiny brow knitted with concentration as she worked on Jool's breast. But Jool and I were also having a bit of an argument.

"Hey," I said, "you'll be nursing her at least another year! You can't be part of it! You have to sit this one out."

"Forget that. I'm her model, Curtis. I'm her mother figure! And she's gonna know that her momma fought back."

"You've already fought through two shoots! She'll know you fought back. She'll see it on-screen whenever she wants."

"I don't want her seeing either one of those fucking vids!"

"Well, which is it? You want her to know you fought back or not?"

"I want her to know I paid those fuckers back for what they did to us. I don't want her seeing any Live Action, and anyway there won't be any vid of what we do to those fuckers, but I want her to know I helped do it to 'em."

I pretended to chew on that for a while because I wasn't going to budge her now anyway, and I had till next spring to convince her. But I couldn't help answering. "What are you saying? There won't be any vid of what we do to them? They won't shoot it? We won't? Kate Harlow's working on it as we speak."

"Just because I let you get me pregnant doesn't mean you can keep me out of the fight."

"We got you pregnant, hon, come on! I just think—"

"Just go away, Curtis. Leave us alone. You're disturbing her lunchtime!"

"I'm not disturbing her! Look how she's scarfing away!"

But seeing Jool's glower, I grabbed my coat and got scarce.

I gave a whistle and Chance—we hadn't changed his name—came wagging along.

I stood out there thinking I might take our little snowcat down into town—all the rolling slopes white, the dark trees in fur coats of powder. . . . Then thought I was being a wuss, and decided to hike down. Crunch and slog through the drifts—be one with the planet.

I started well, but slipping became an issue on the steeper slopes. I left a number of skid-marks and butt-prints behind me. Anyone who wanted to track me would have no problem, if they could stop laughing. Snow looks so dry somehow, at least to a novice. It's amazing how wet it can get you, and amazing how cold you can get when you're wet.

But somehow, just after my hands and my feet had gone totally numb, I did feel at one with the planet. Nothing smarmy about it either, that feeling. These peaks here I was crossing the flanks of, stuck straight up into the universe. At night, there was nothing but space between them and the stars.

And I couldn't help thinking the game that I and my friends were preparing to play was a Ghoul's Dance to perform for our neighbors, the galaxies. Yet it was our dance to do, and do it we would with all of our strength. . . .

Ten minutes later I had Sunrise in sight below me. Our town had a bigger profile now. Up behind the industrial zone there were two big new warehouse structures—one of them the hangar that housed our growing fleet of antigravs, and the other an armory-*cum* weapons plant.

I went straight down into town to the Cuppa Joe, where I found Japh and Chops and Ricky Dawes slumped comfortably at the coffee bar with steaming mugs in front of them. I took the stool beside Japh.

"Suzy, my sylph," I said, "a cup of the same for me, please."

Suzy was my height, and a pretty tough customer. "Not till you tell me what a sylph is," she said.

"A woodland spirit."

"That and two-fifty will do it."

After a warming gulp, I asked my friends, "So. How's our box-office boys?"

Worn though the joke was, it always made us laugh. *Assault on Sunrise Uncut* had hit the market a whole month before *Assault on Sunrise* itself. Margolian's third of a billion was far less than half of Sunrise Incorporated's total wealth now, and the torrent of revenues just kept rushing in.

But it happened, with the wintry light coming in the windows, that our laughter at that moment had an after-echo. A silence fell, and in it we heard faraway echos of voices we would never hear again. We didn't fight the feeling. The silence drew out, and we let it.

I noticed Ricky's eyes were wet. He wiped them. "I always thought I had a bad memory," he said, and cleared his throat. "But I can remember all their faces so sharp, remember things they said. We were, like, robbed of them!"

"We're gonna rob those fuckers back, Ricky," Chops said. "It's not enough, but it's something."

"I've been reading about Hitler," Japh told us quietly. "About his *Festung Europa* once he'd conquered his neighbors and barricaded his borders. Fortress Europe, he called it."

I cleared my throat. "And maybe you were also thinking . . . of Fortress Hollywood?"

"Indeed I was, Curtis, indeed I was."

"Whaddaya mean, Fortress Europe?" Ricky asked.

"Europe, you know," Japh said. "All those countries across the Atlantic Ocean? Hitler had 'em barricaded against his enemies, who were basically us and England. And by the time we were through with him, his fortress was, like, smoking rubble."

"You mean like, all exploded?" he asked in a rusty voice.

"That's what I mean." Japh told him.

"Fortress Hollywood," Ricky mused. "Smoking rubble. Man, that would be something!"